OPHELIA HOUSE

NO WORRIES

ORIGINAL ARTWORK

ANDREW L. WILLIS

CREATED AND WRITTEN

CARLTON L. SAMPSON
COVER DESIGN, BALLOONS, PAGE LAYOUT

Palanquin

PHILADELPHIA
VETERANS STADIUM

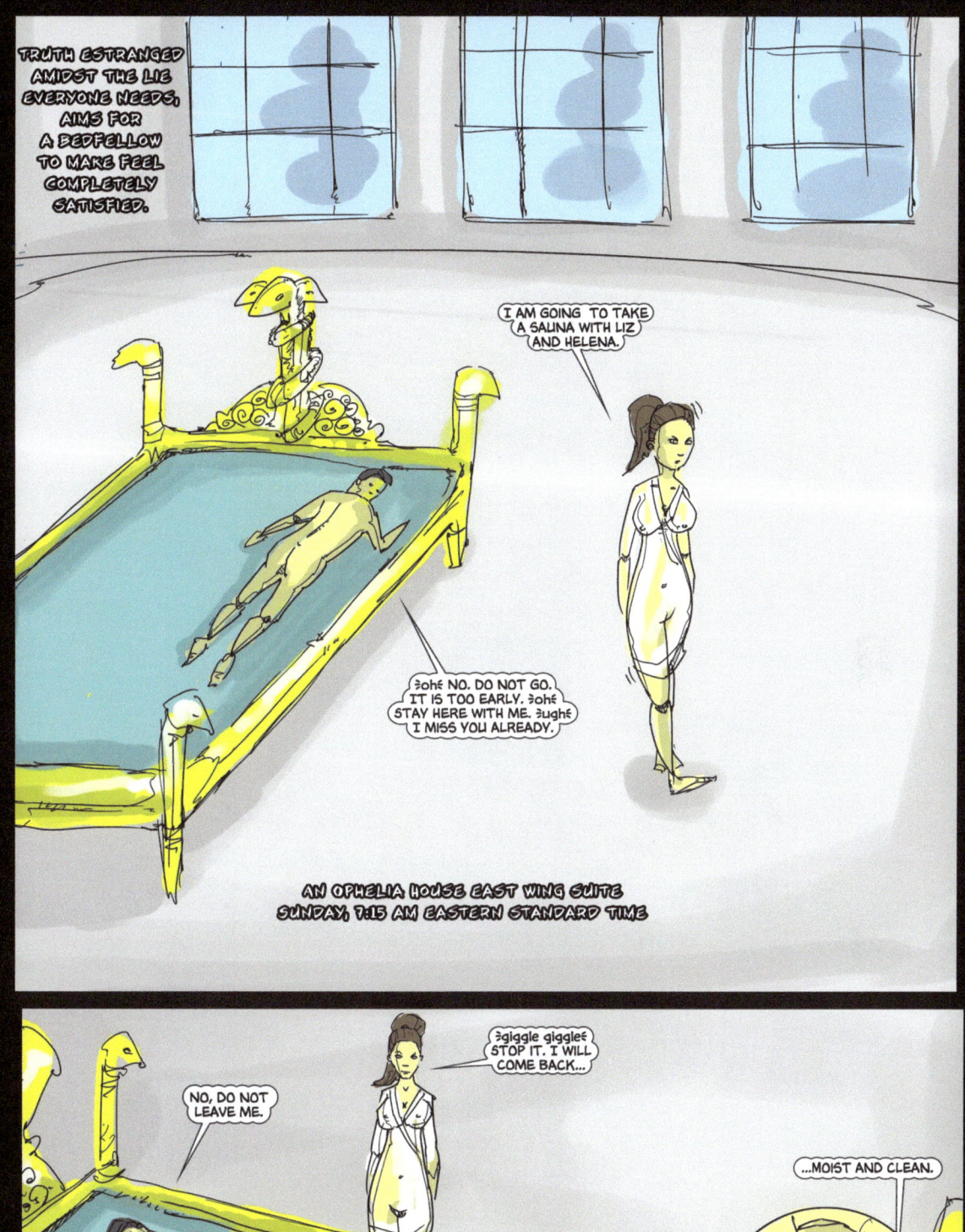

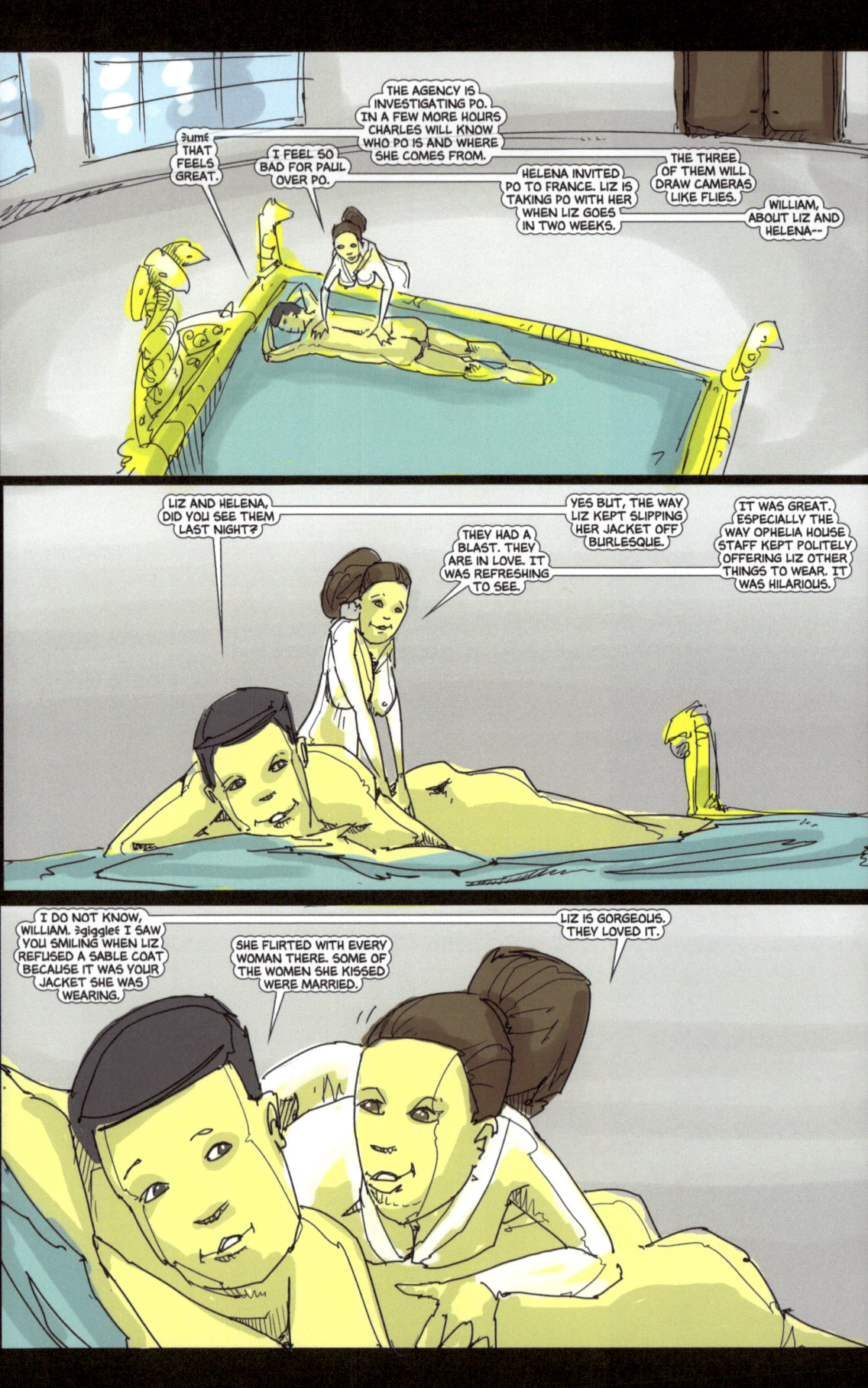

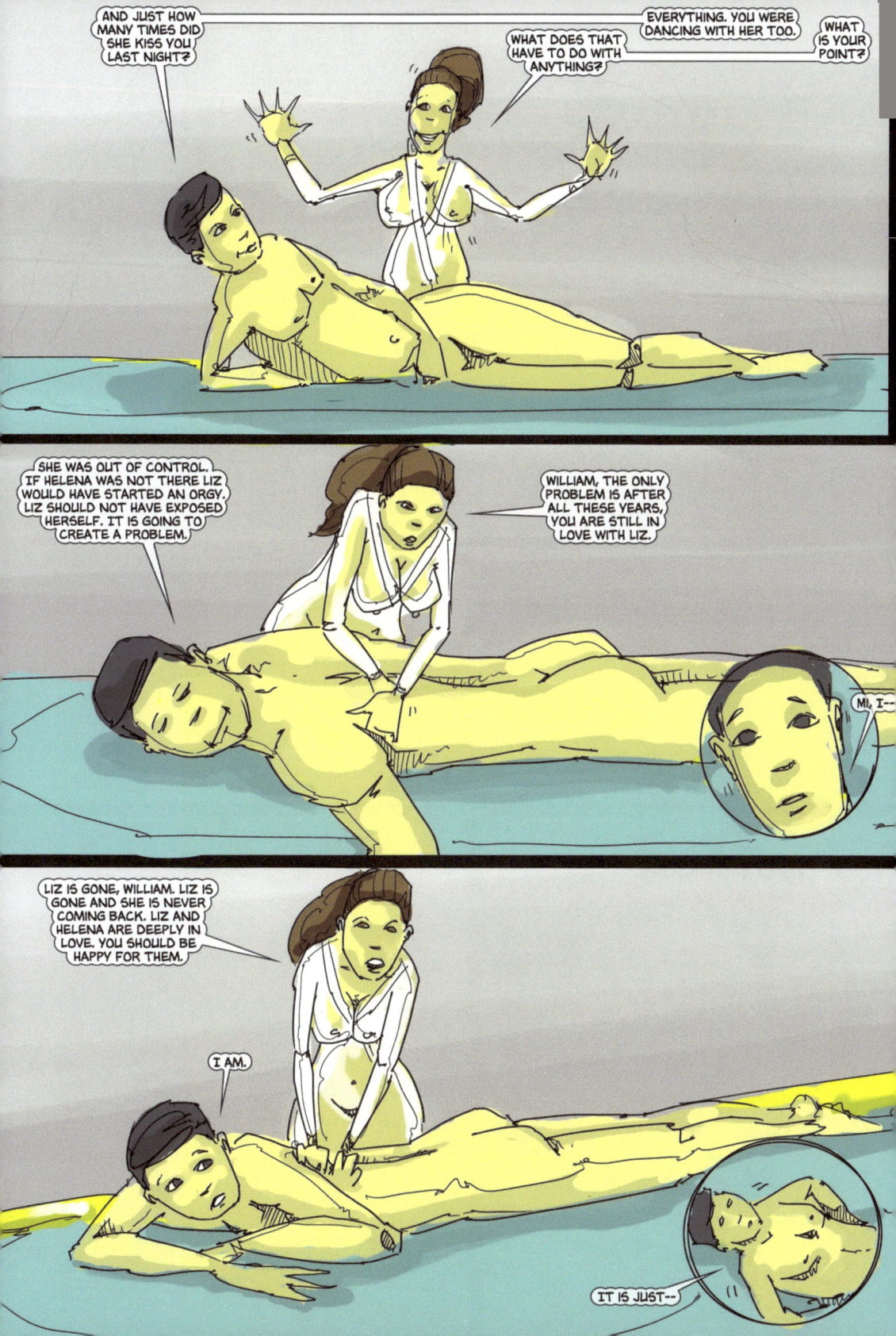

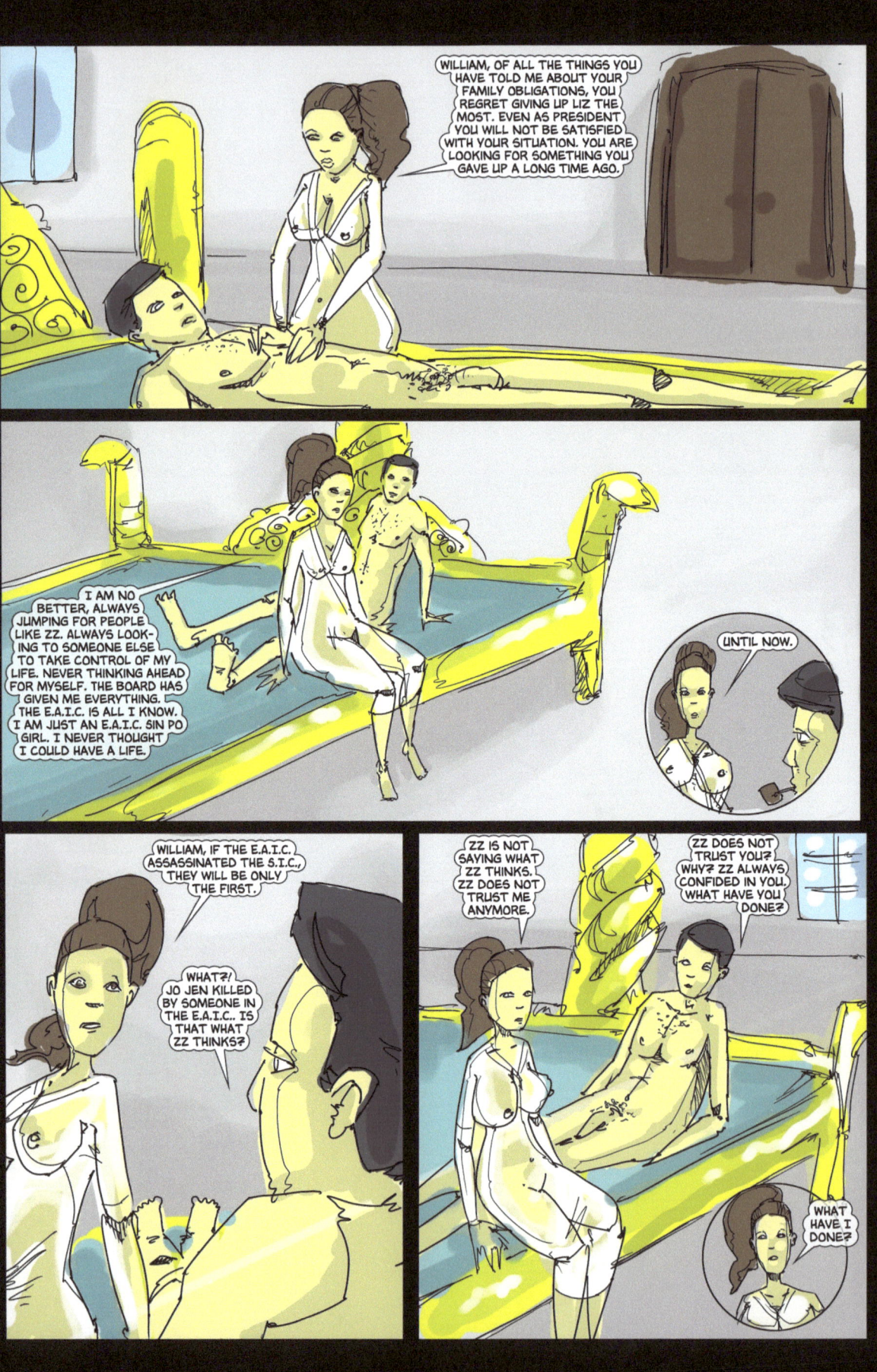

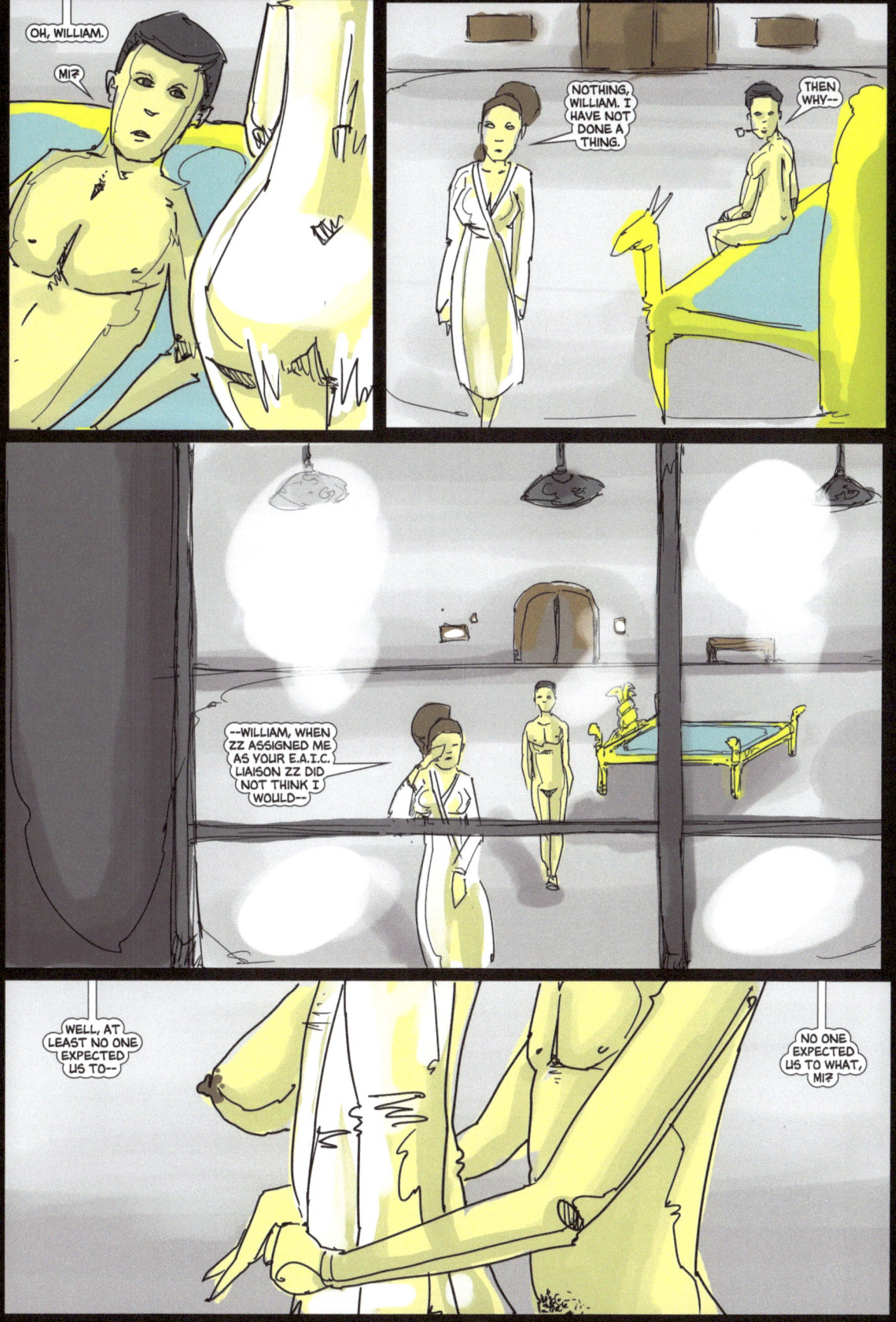

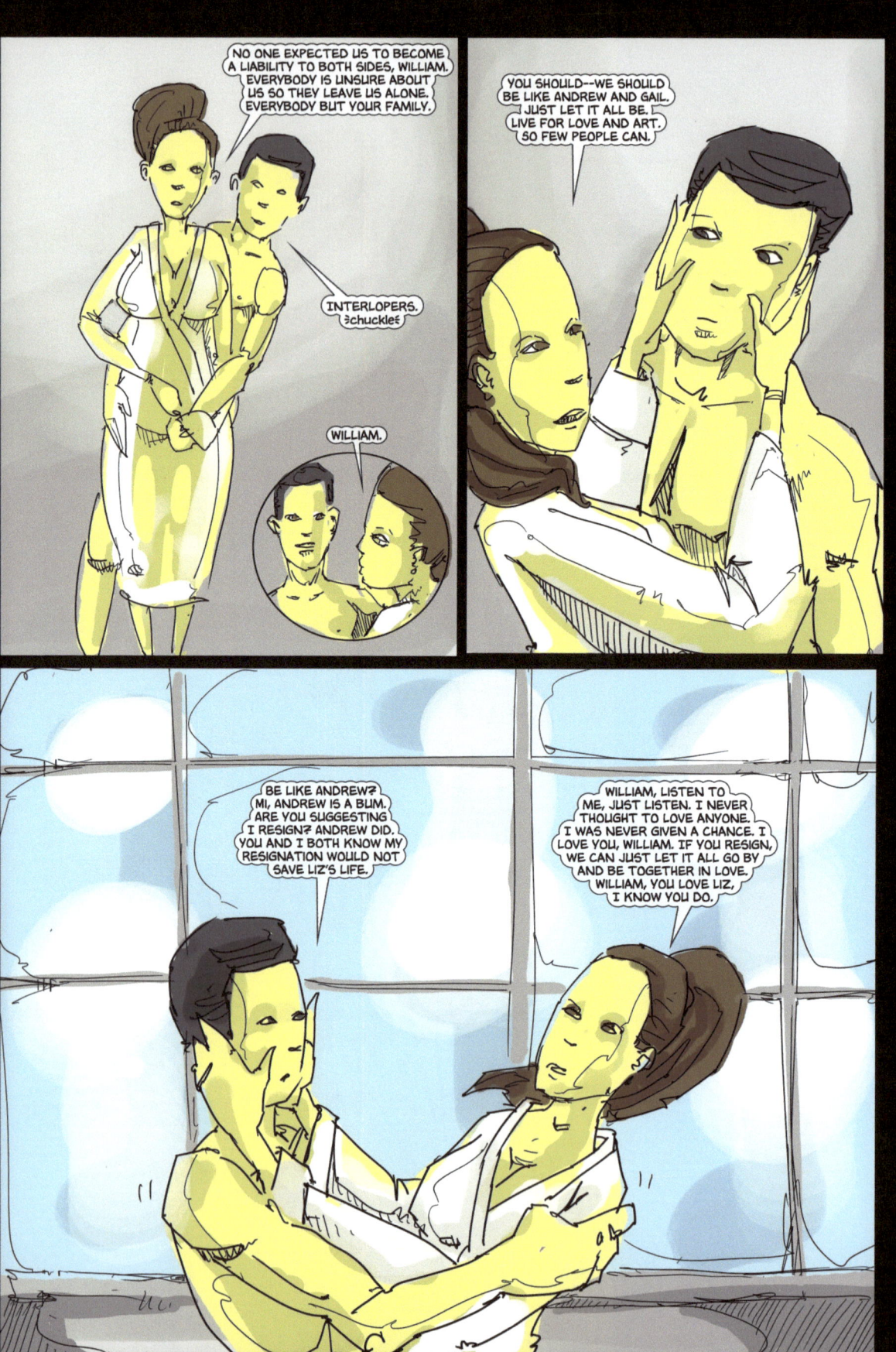

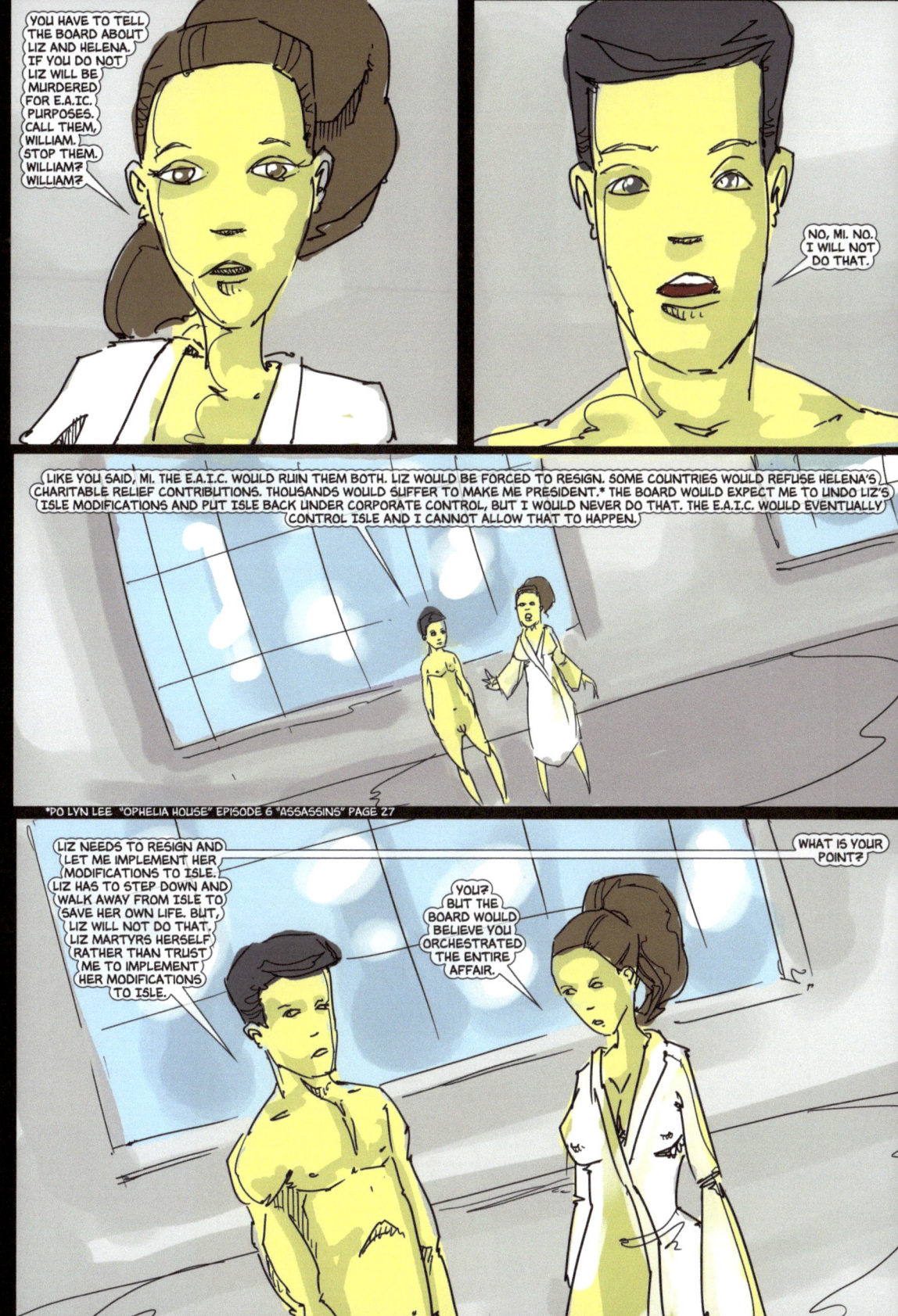

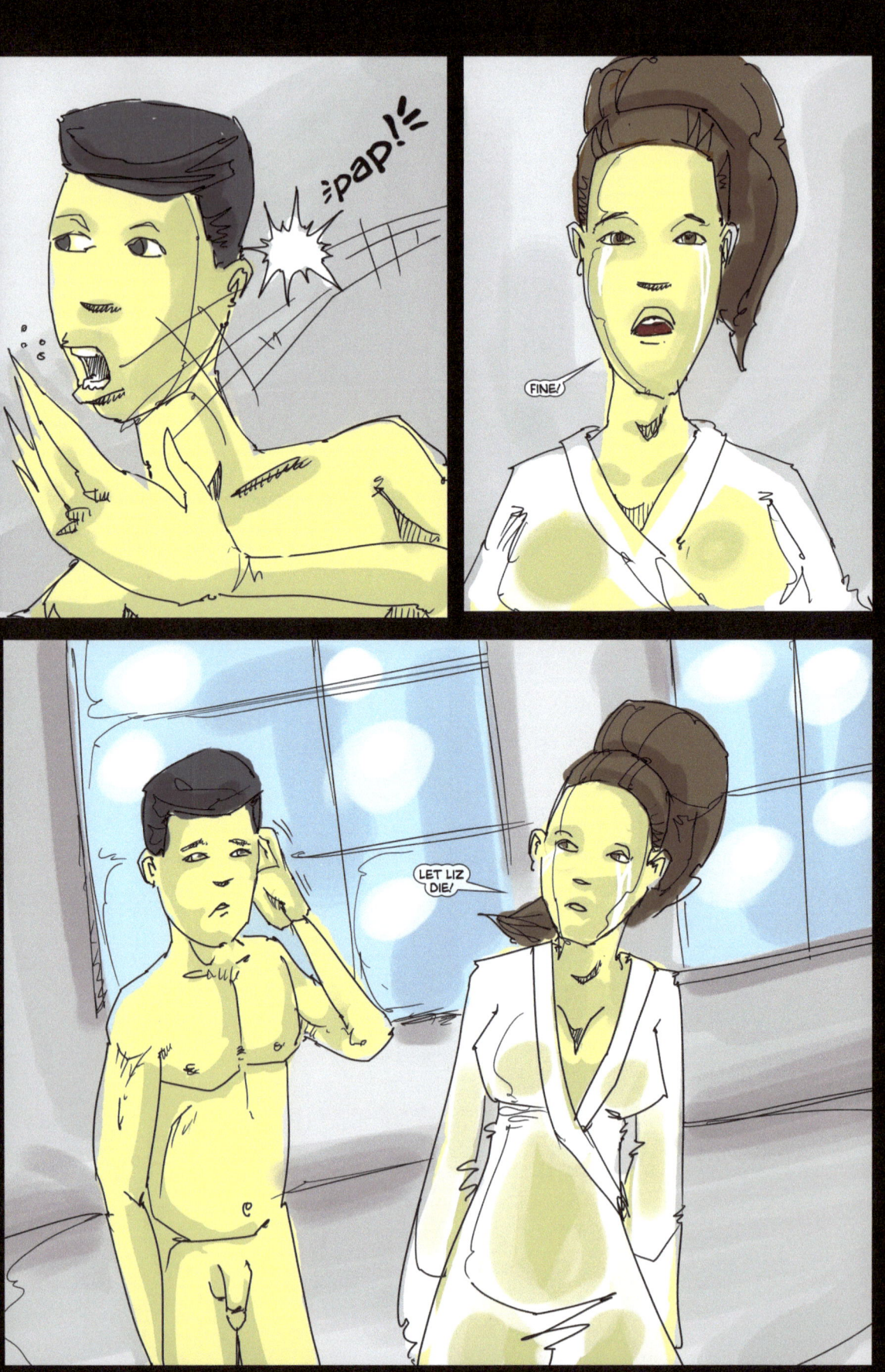

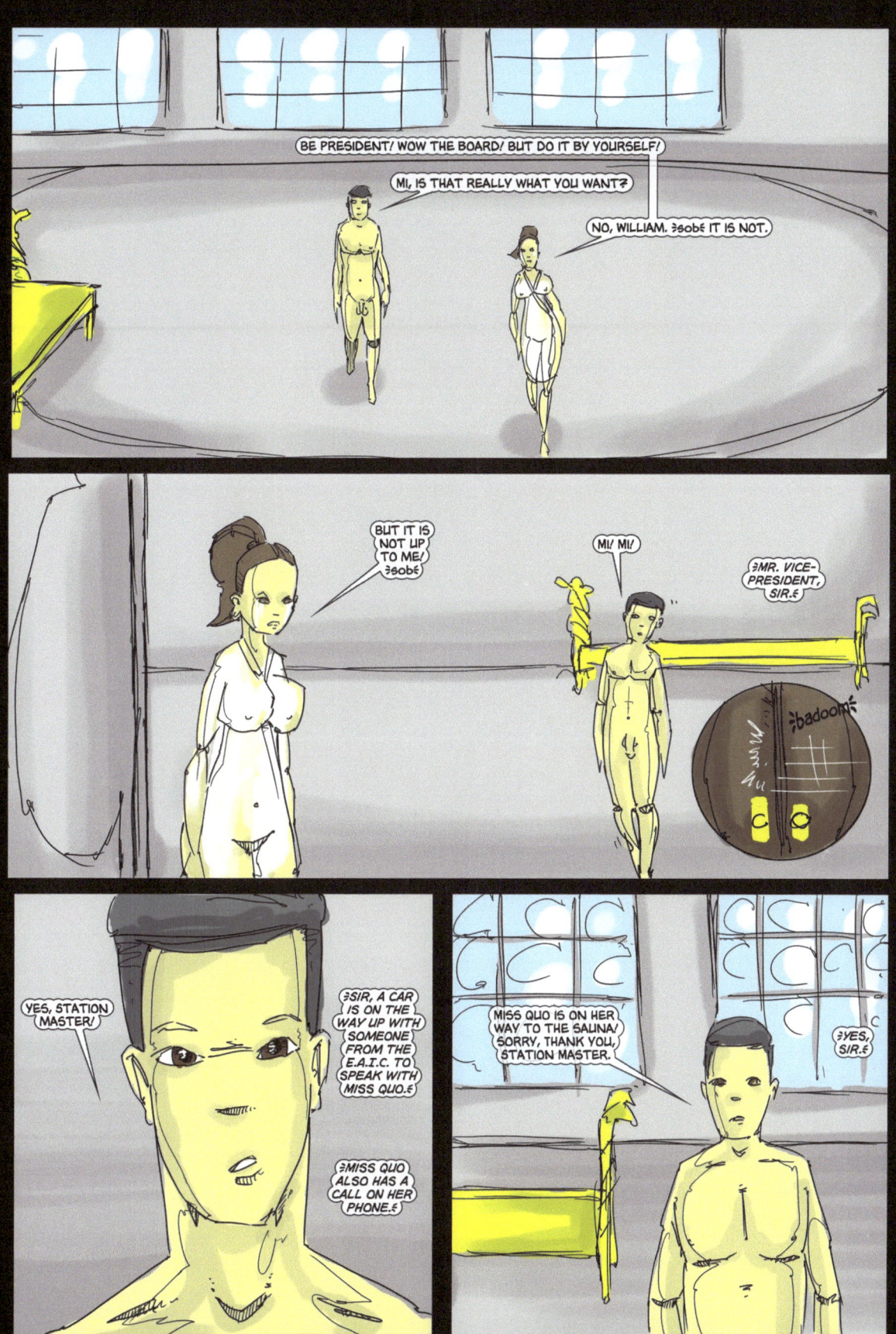

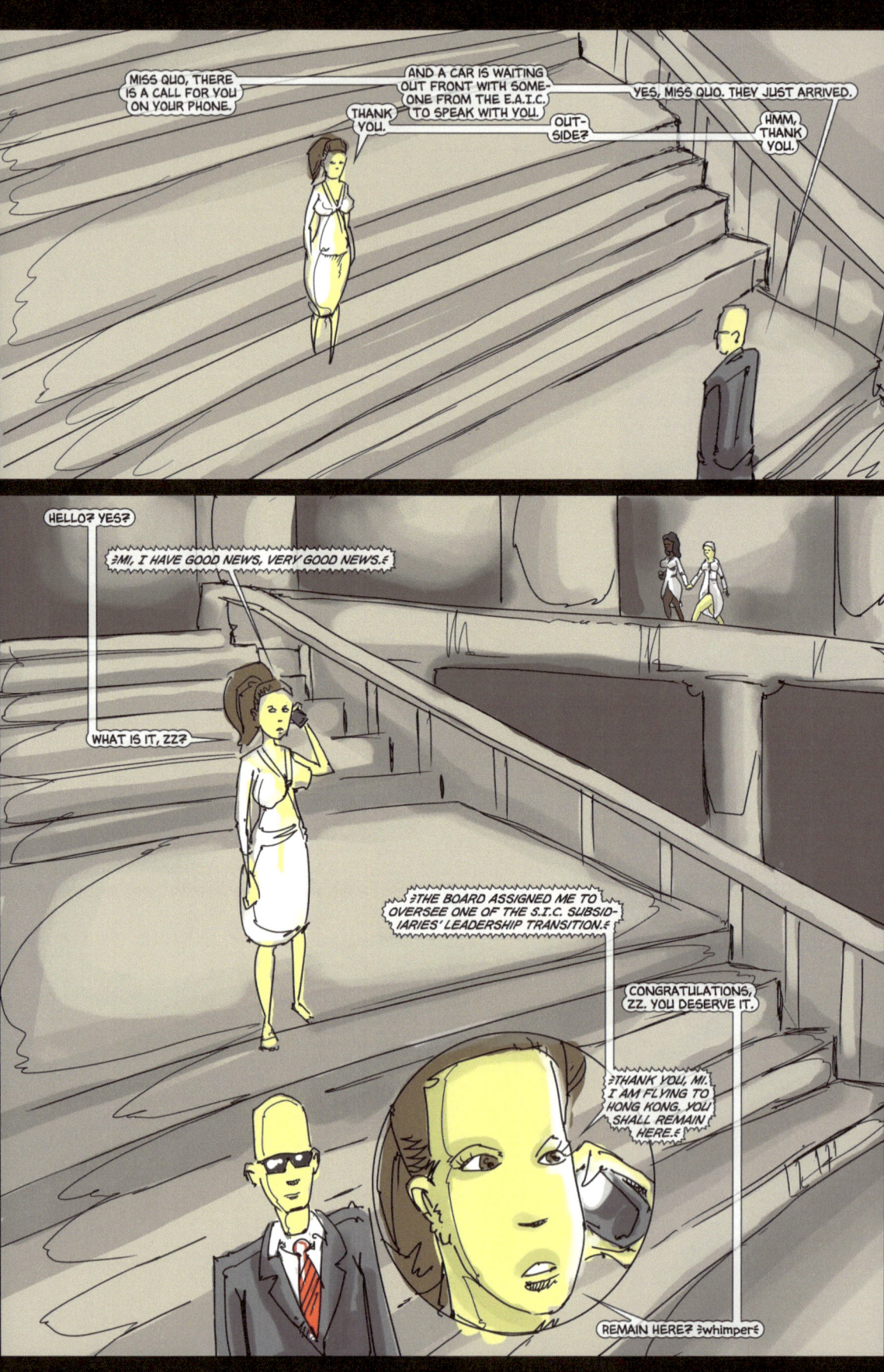

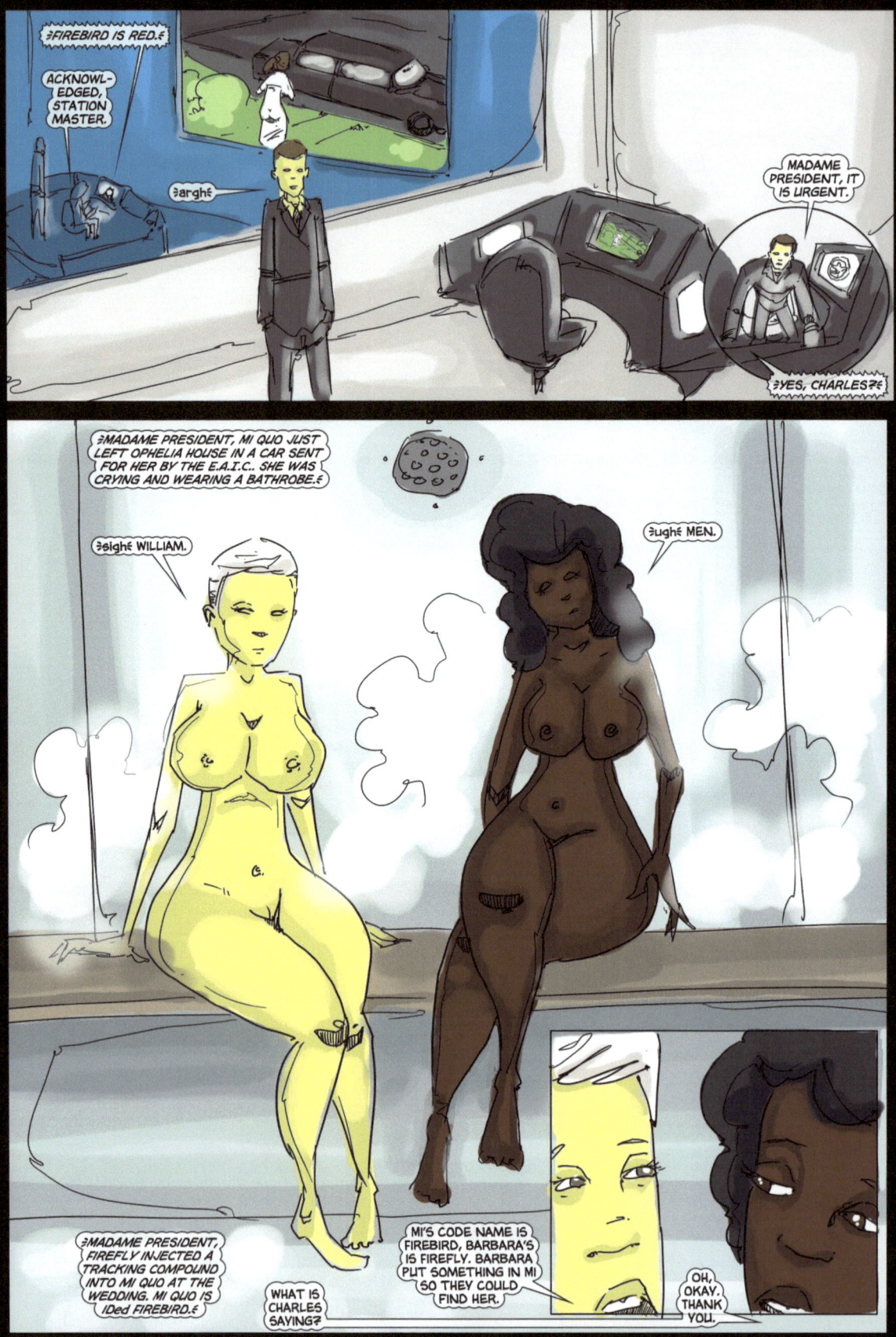

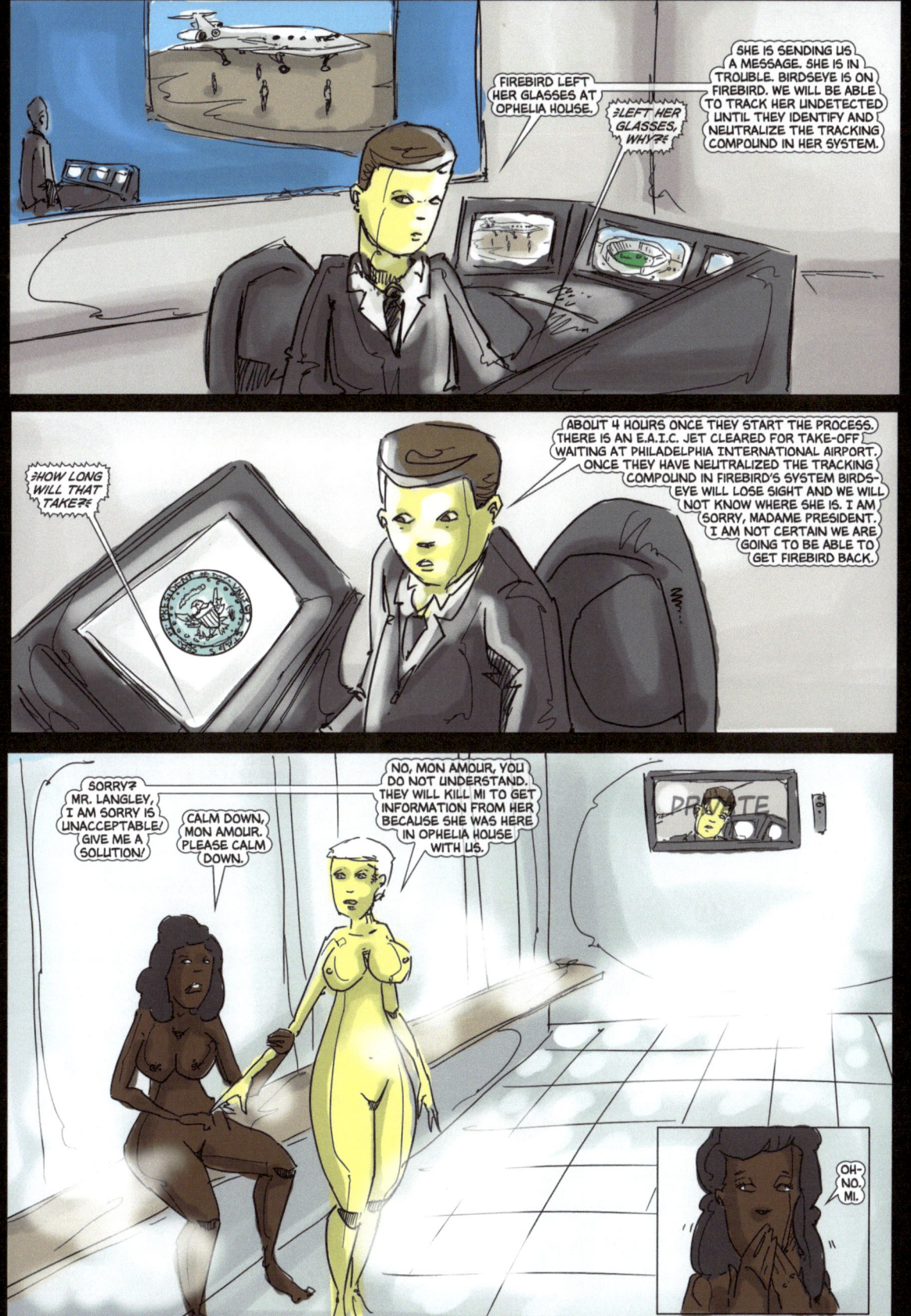

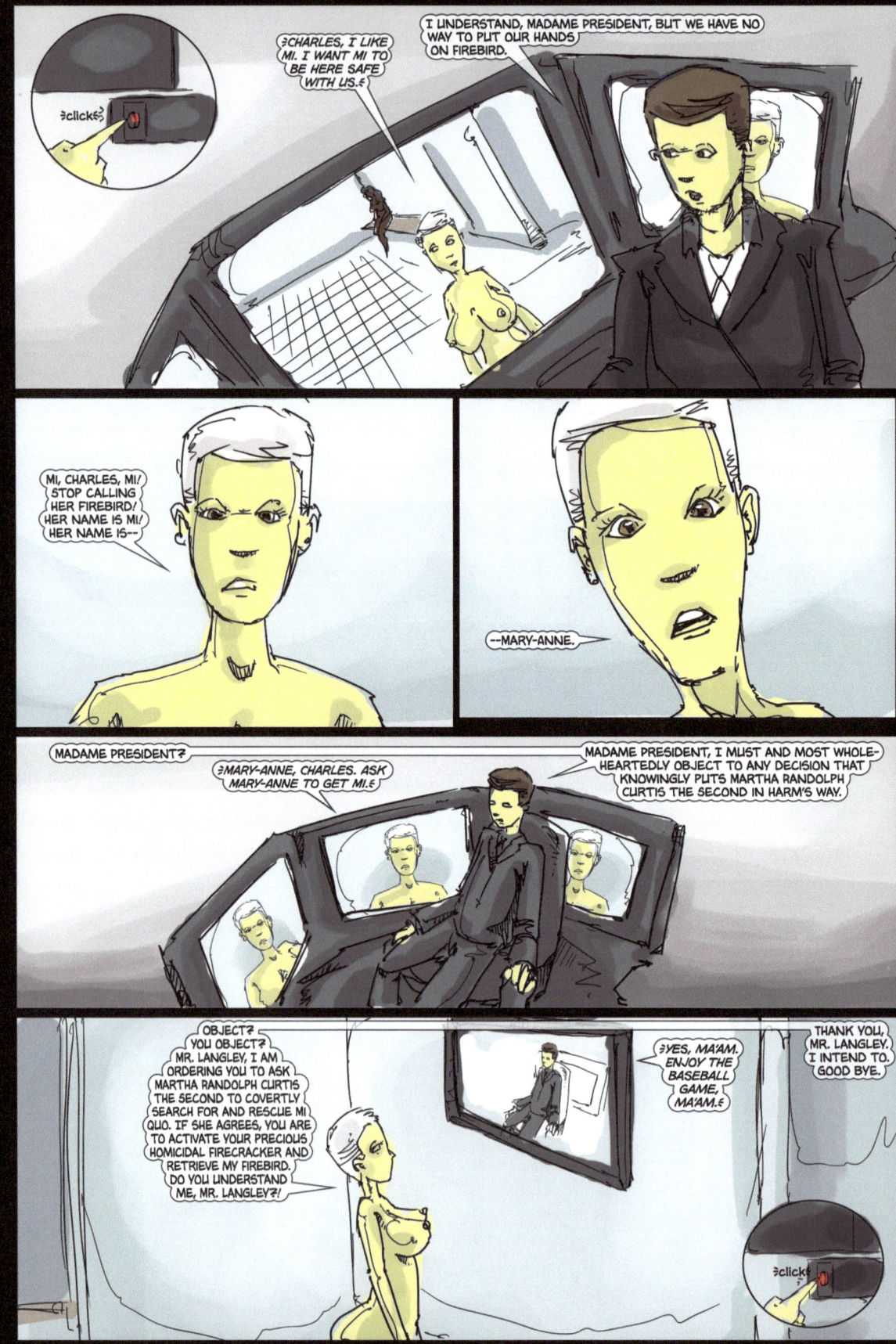

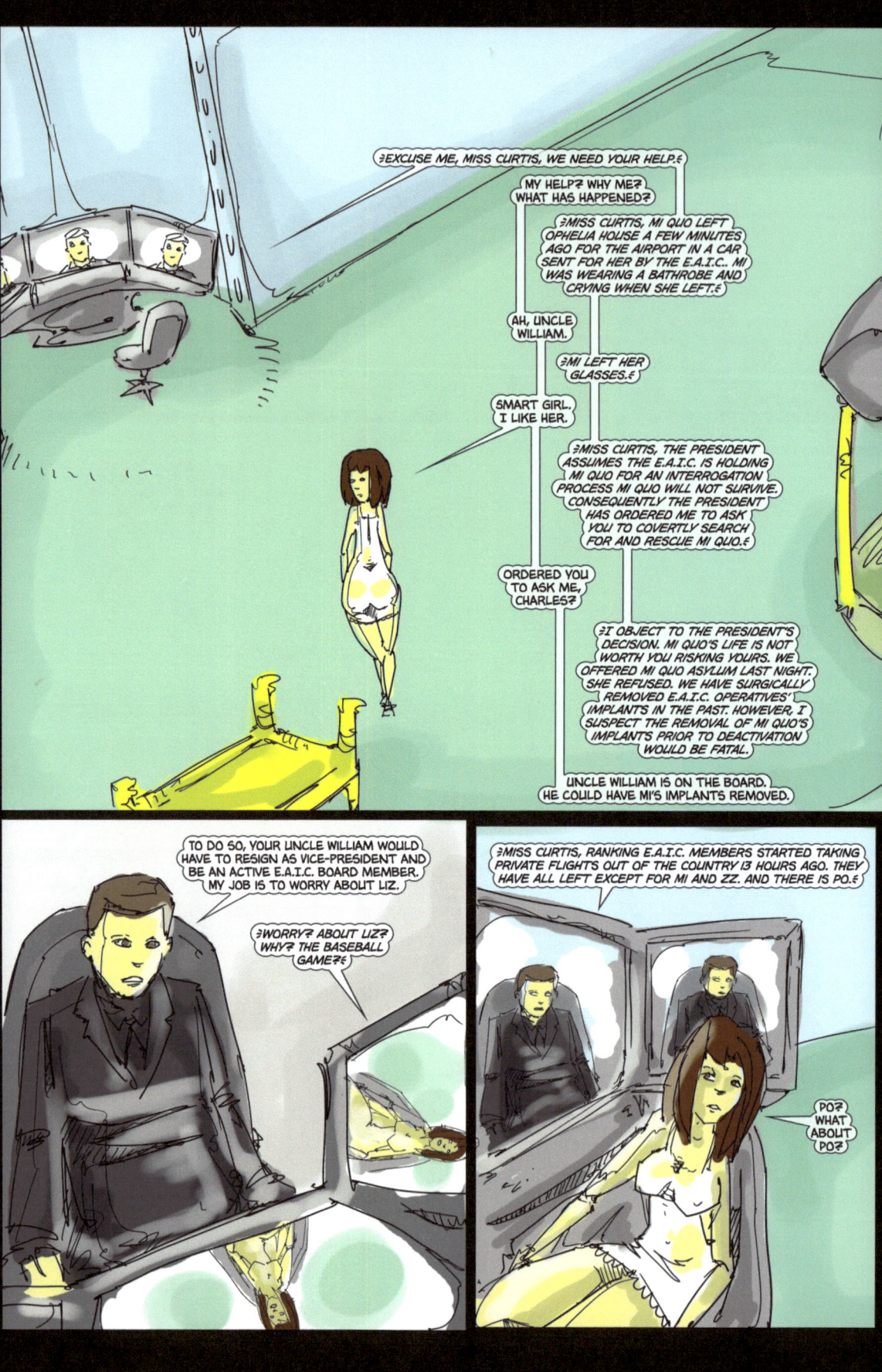

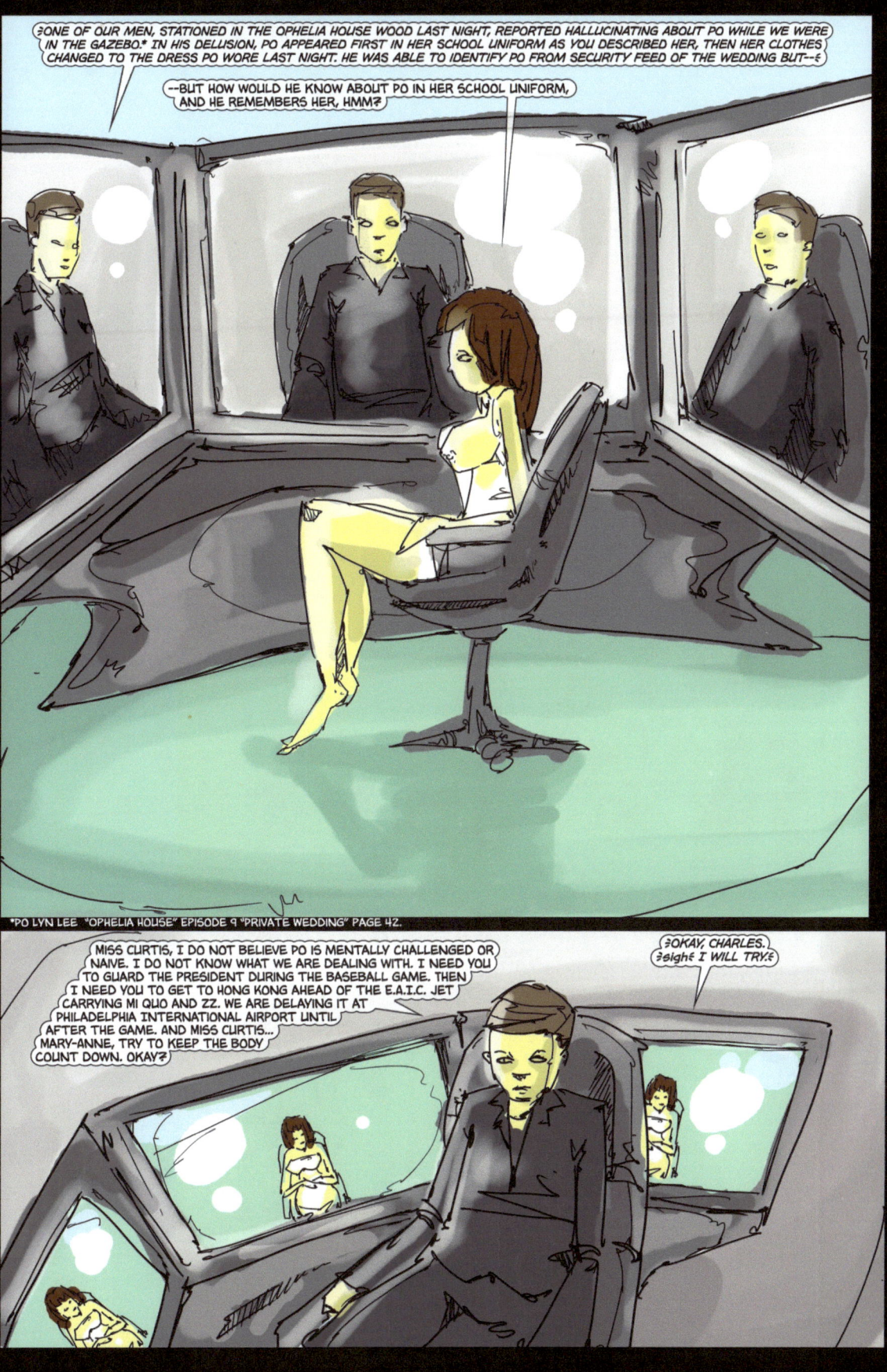

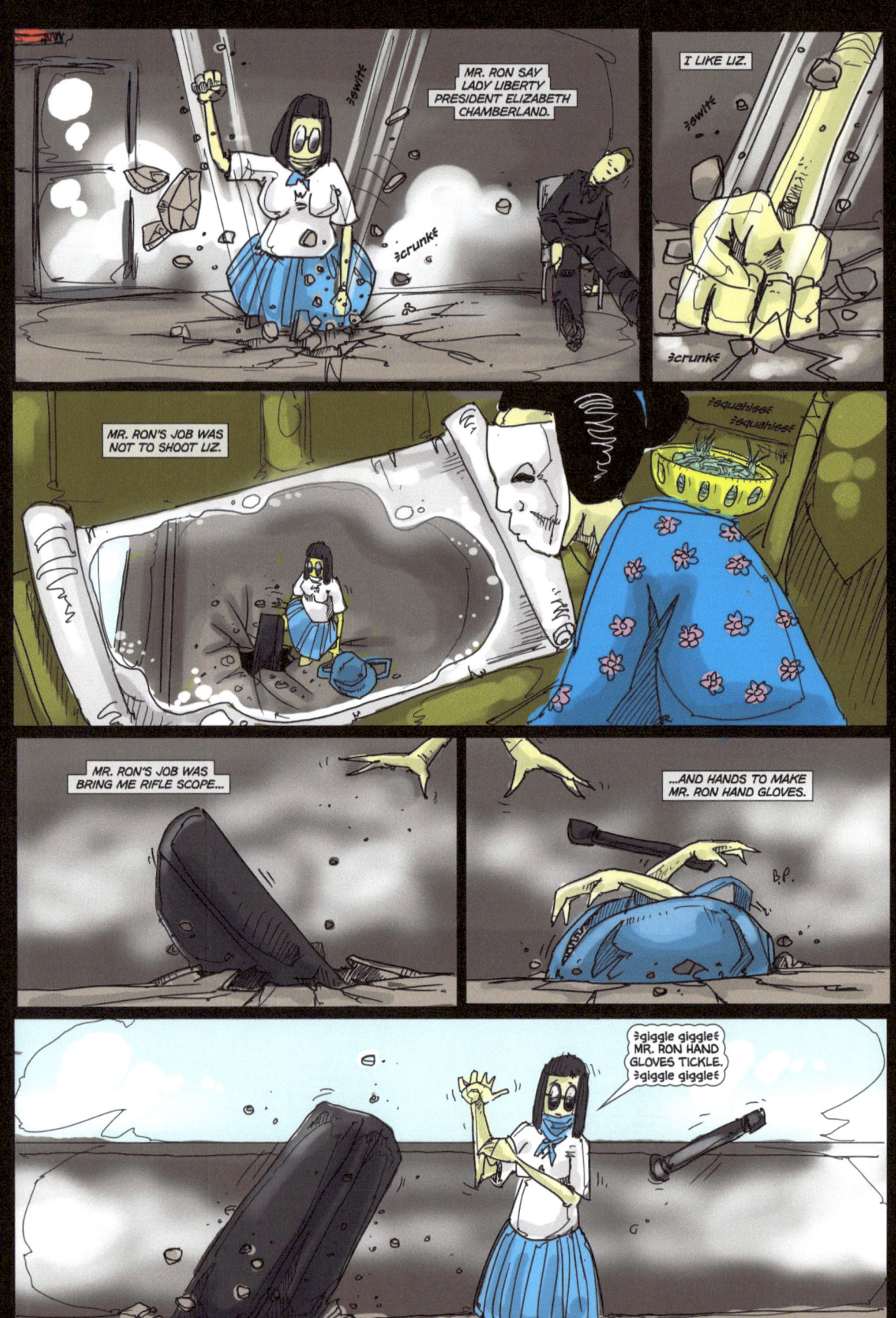

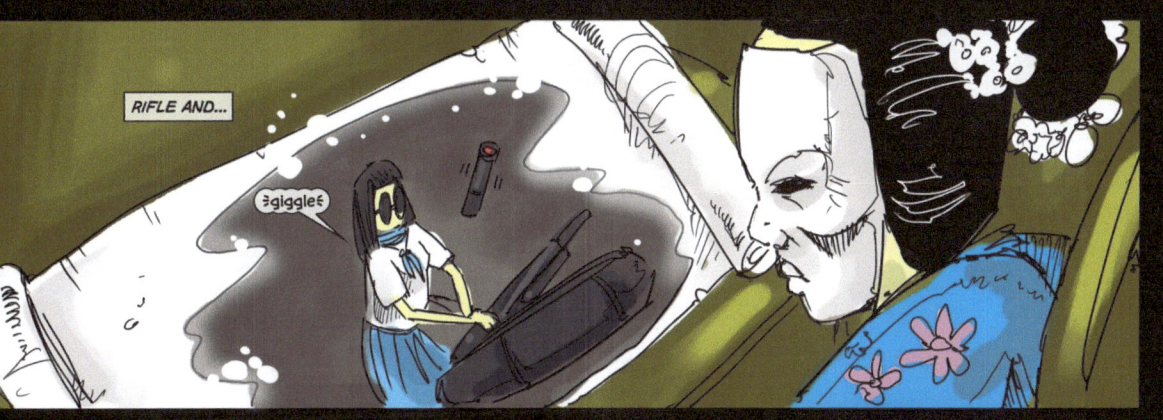

RIFLE AND...

≋giggle≋

...RIFLE SCOPE.

≋giggle≋

MY FAVORITE JOB.

A MESSAGE?

IN RIFLE?

IF YOU SEE MARTHA SHOOT MARTHA FIRST.

IF I SEE MARTHA? HMM?

POP!

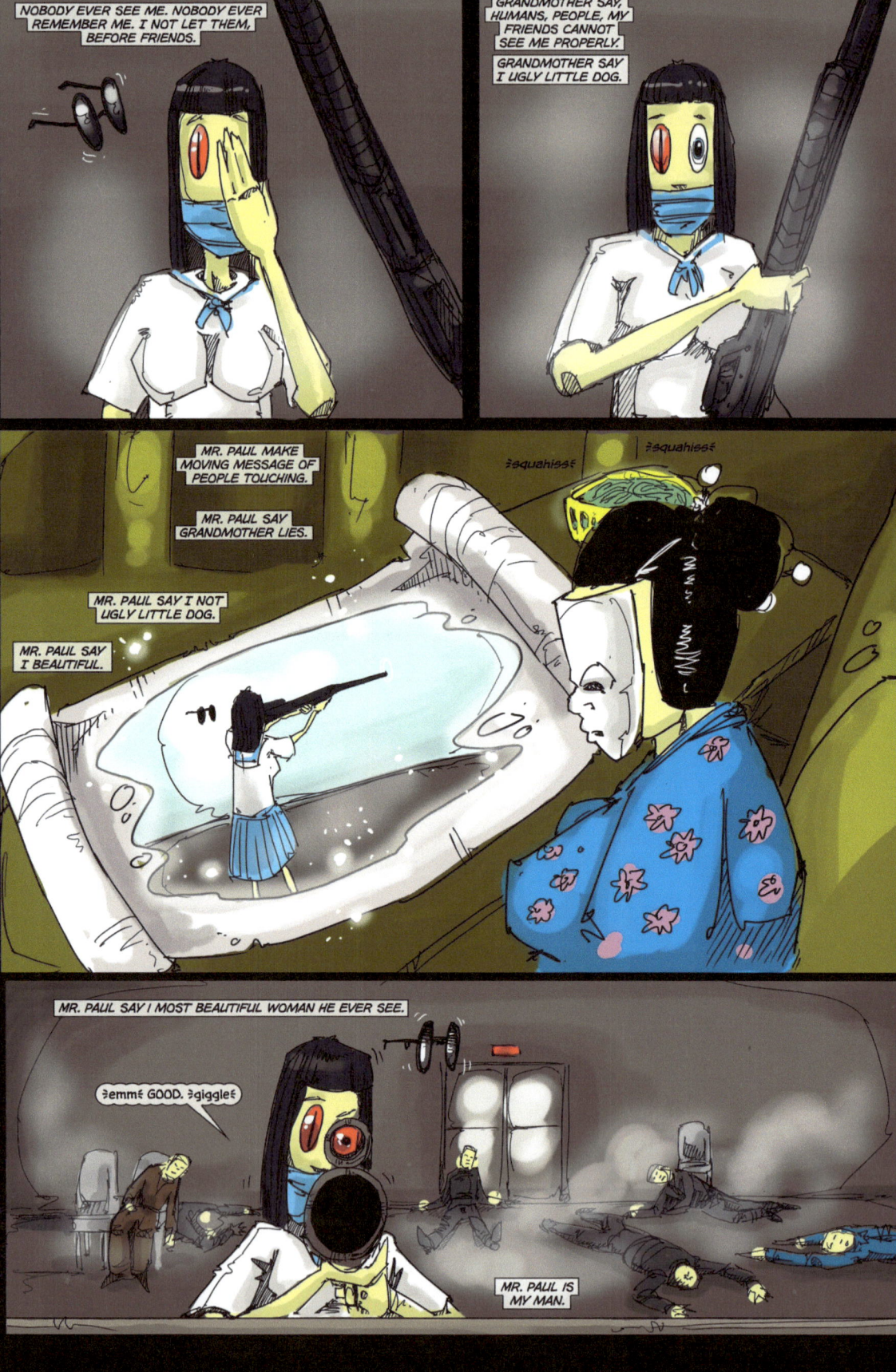

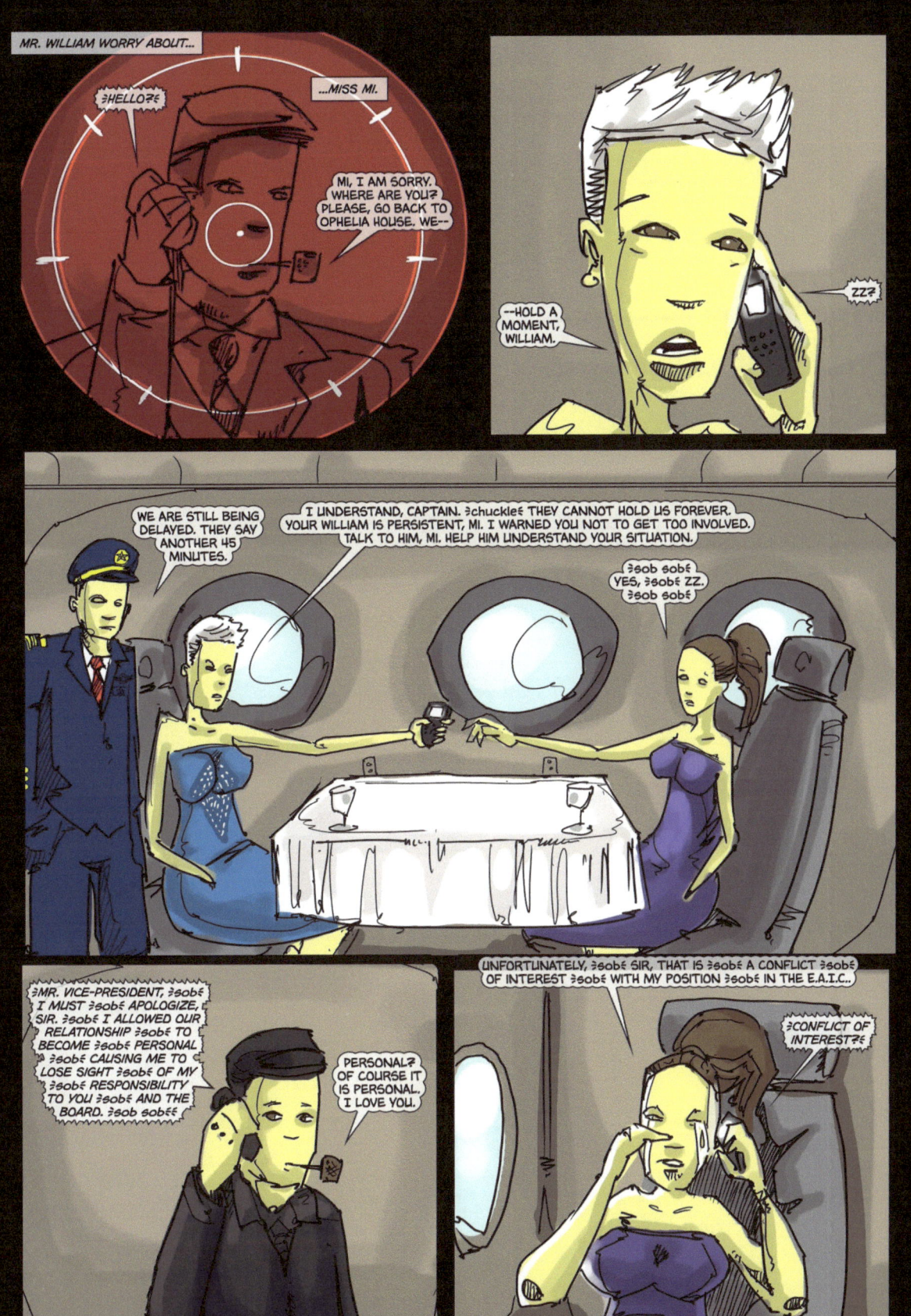

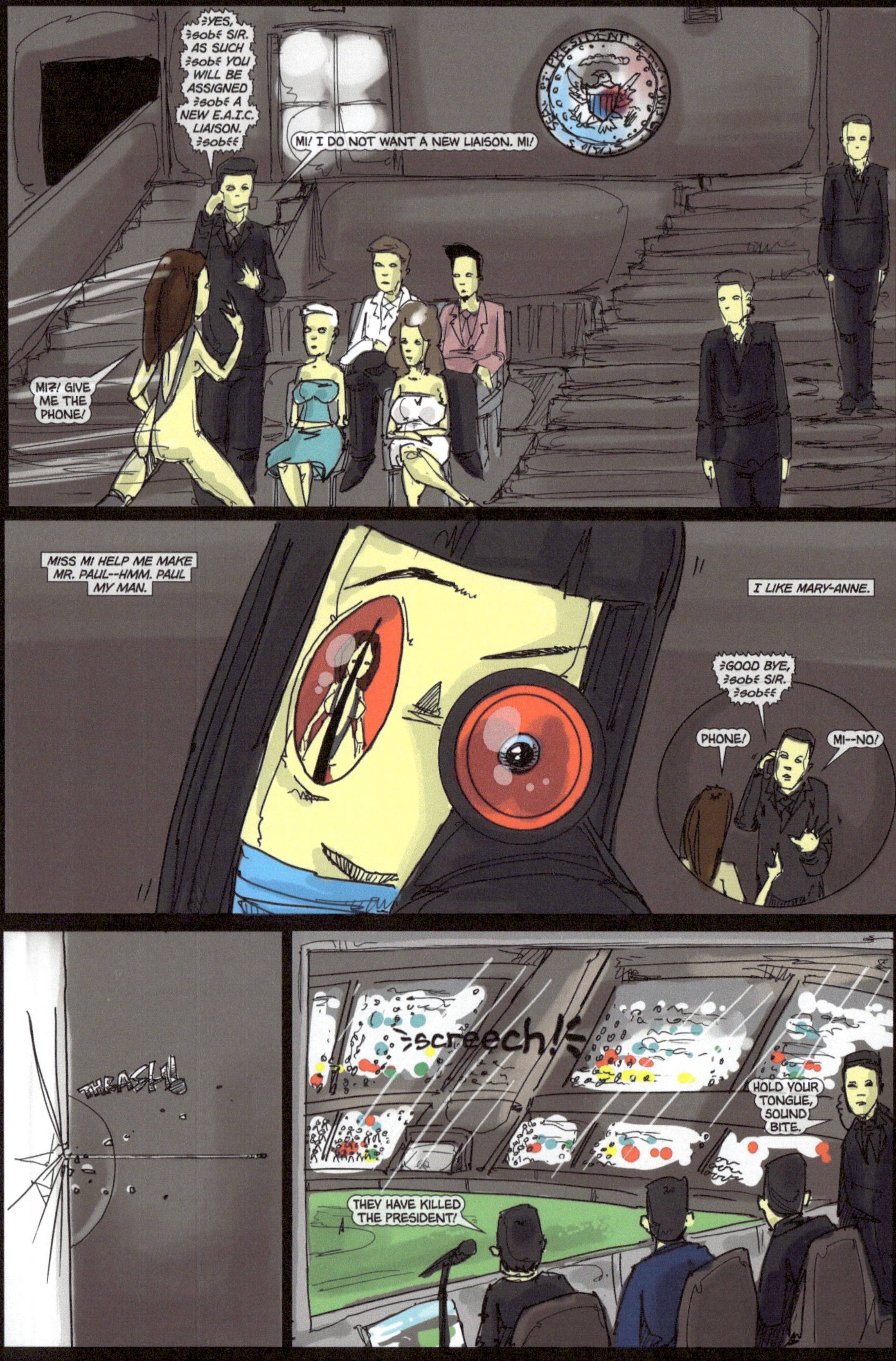

Panel 1:

∋YES, ∋sob∋ SIR. AS SUCH ∋sob∋ YOU WILL BE ASSIGNED ∋sob∋ A NEW E.A.I.C. LIAISON. ∋sob∋∋

MI! I DO NOT WANT A NEW LIAISON. MI!

MI?! GIVE ME THE PHONE!

Panel 2:

MISS MI HELP ME MAKE MR. PAUL--HMM. PAUL MY MAN.

I LIKE MARY-ANNE.

∋GOOD BYE, ∋sob∋ SIR. ∋sob∋∋

PHONE!

MI--NO!

Panel 3:

THRASH!!

Panel 4:

∋screech!∋

HOLD YOUR TONGUE, SOUND BITE.

THEY HAVE KILLED THE PRESIDENT!

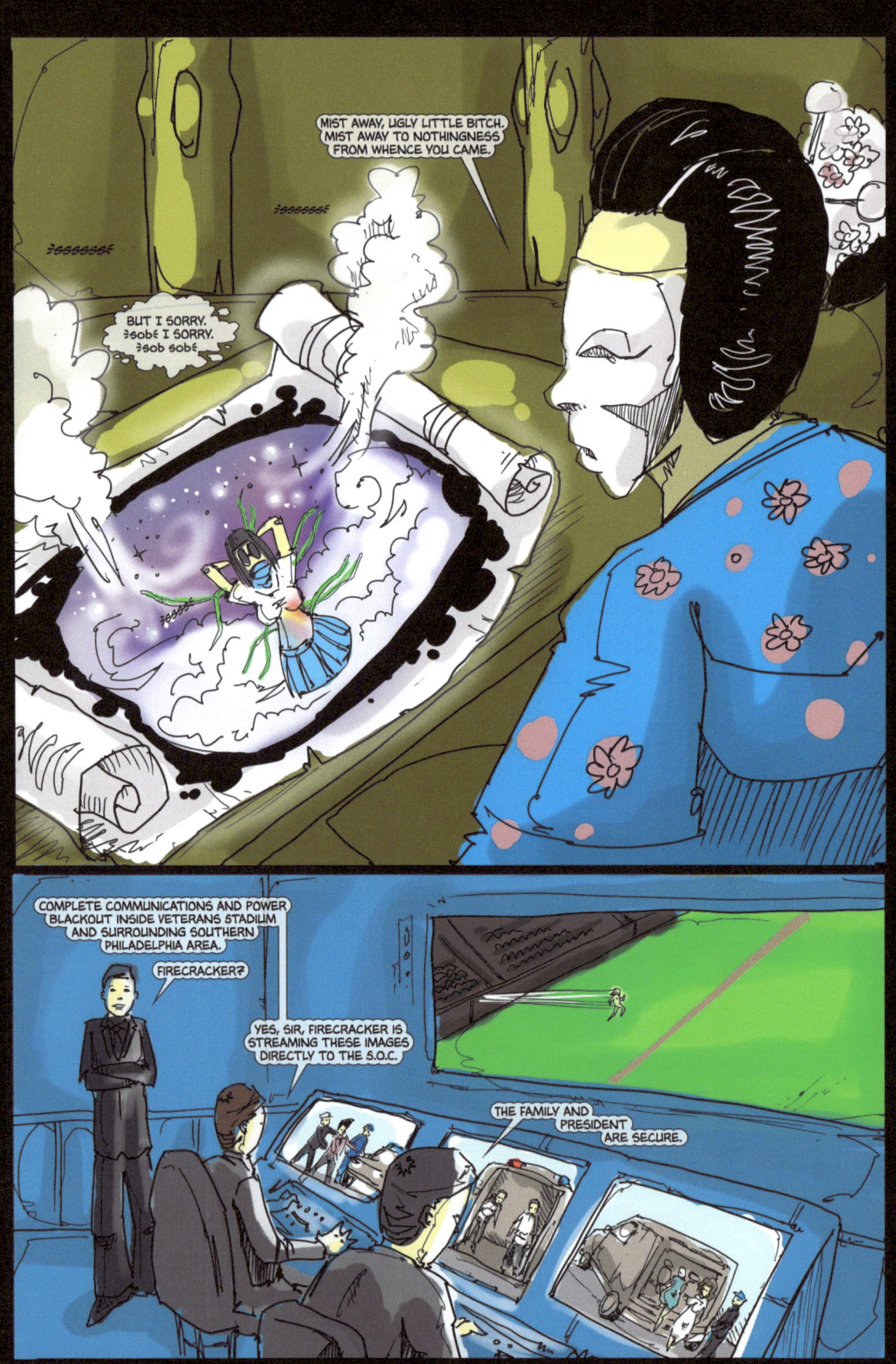

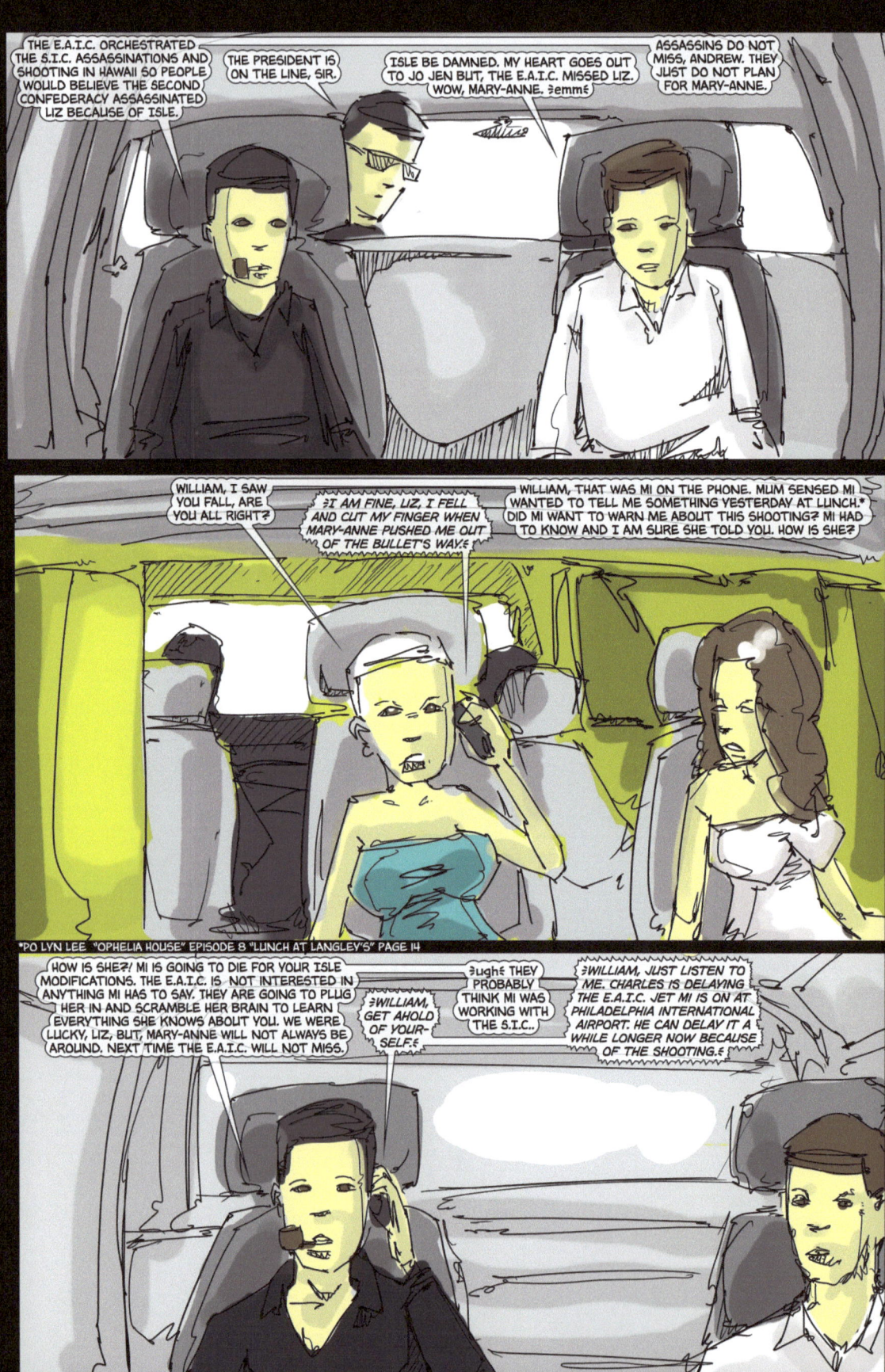

*PO LYN LEE "OPHELIA HOUSE" EPISODE 8 "LUNCH AT LANGLEY'S" PAGE 14

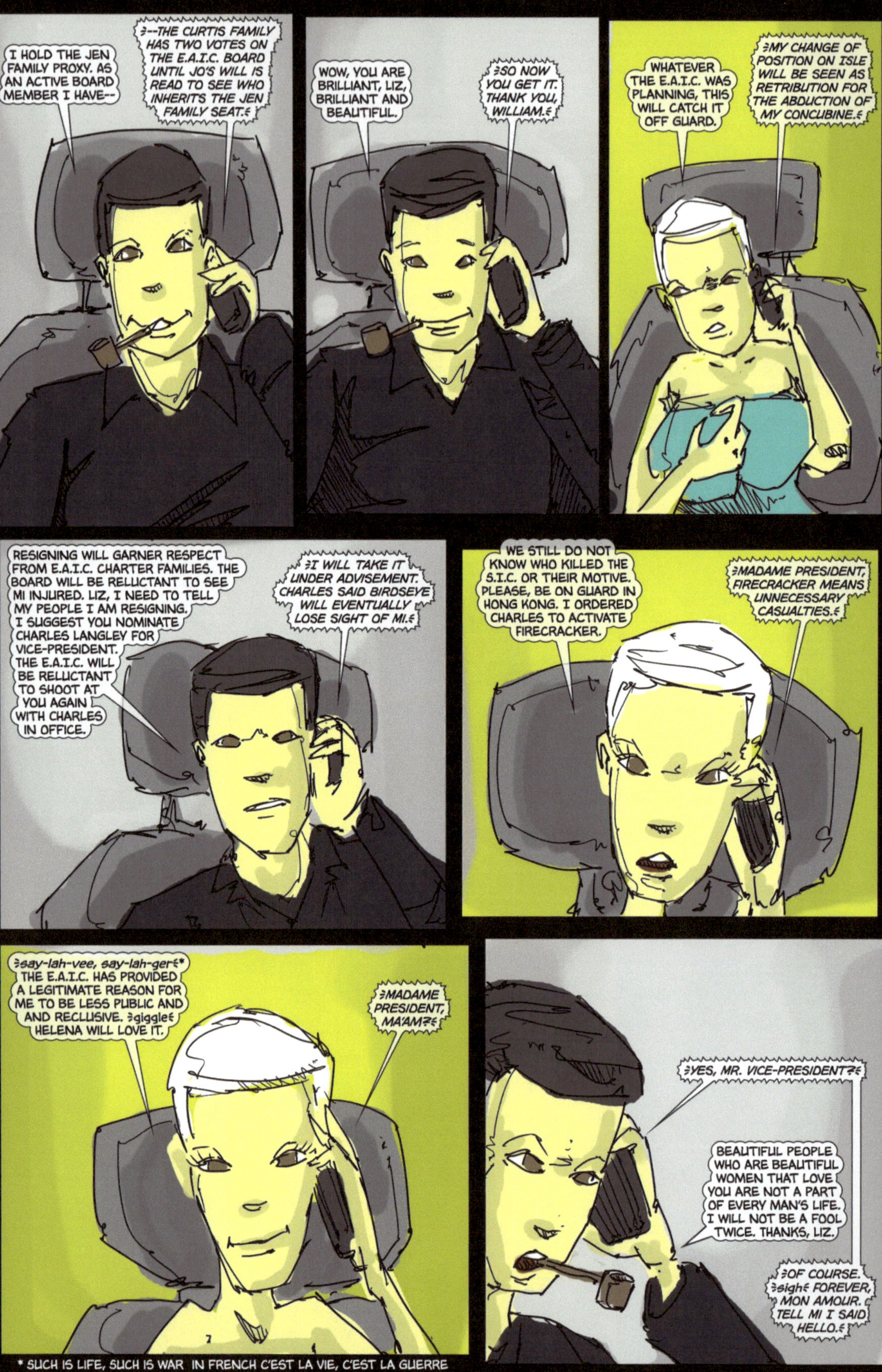

* SUCH IS LIFE, SUCH IS WAR IN FRENCH C'EST LA VIE, C'EST LA GUERRE

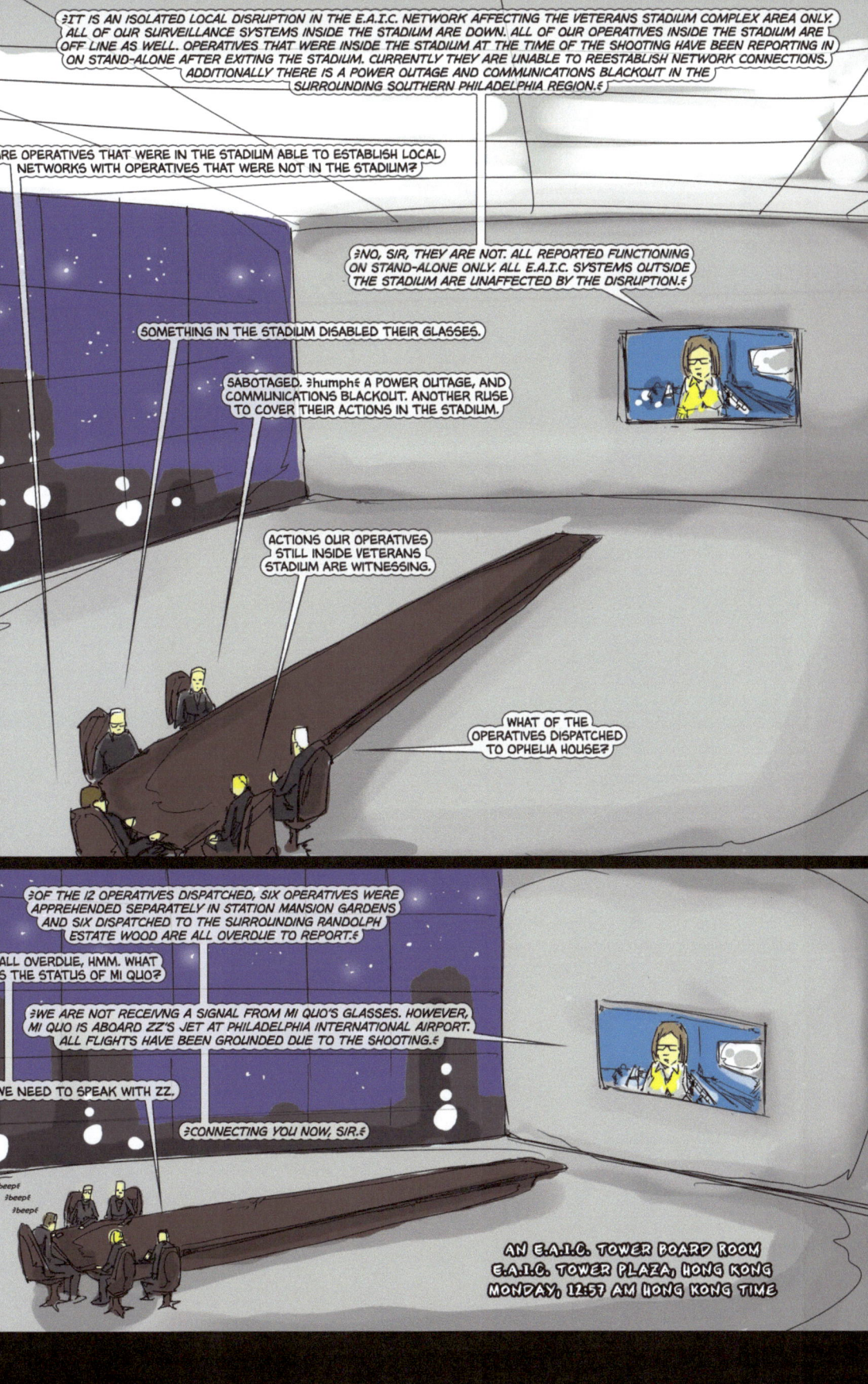

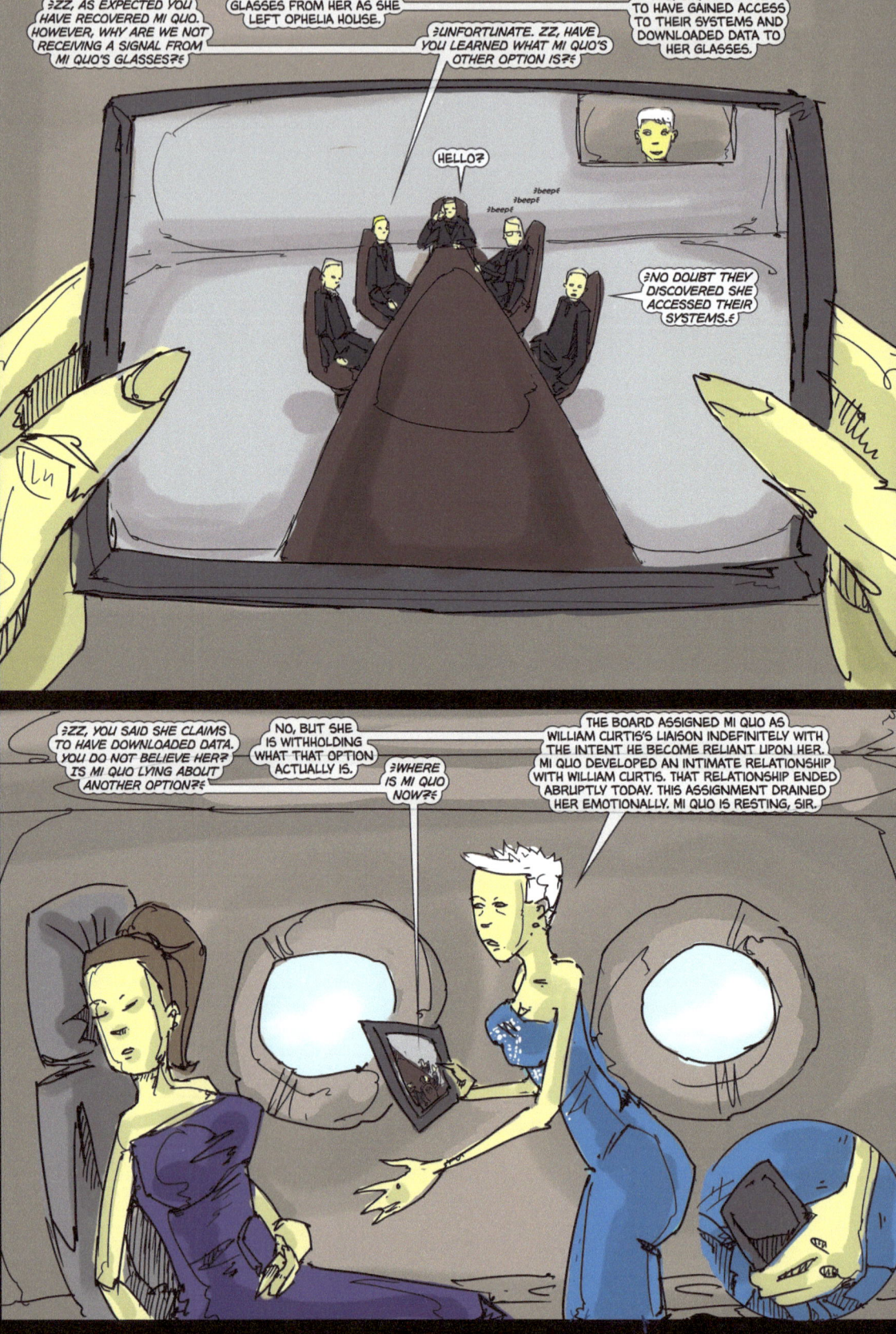

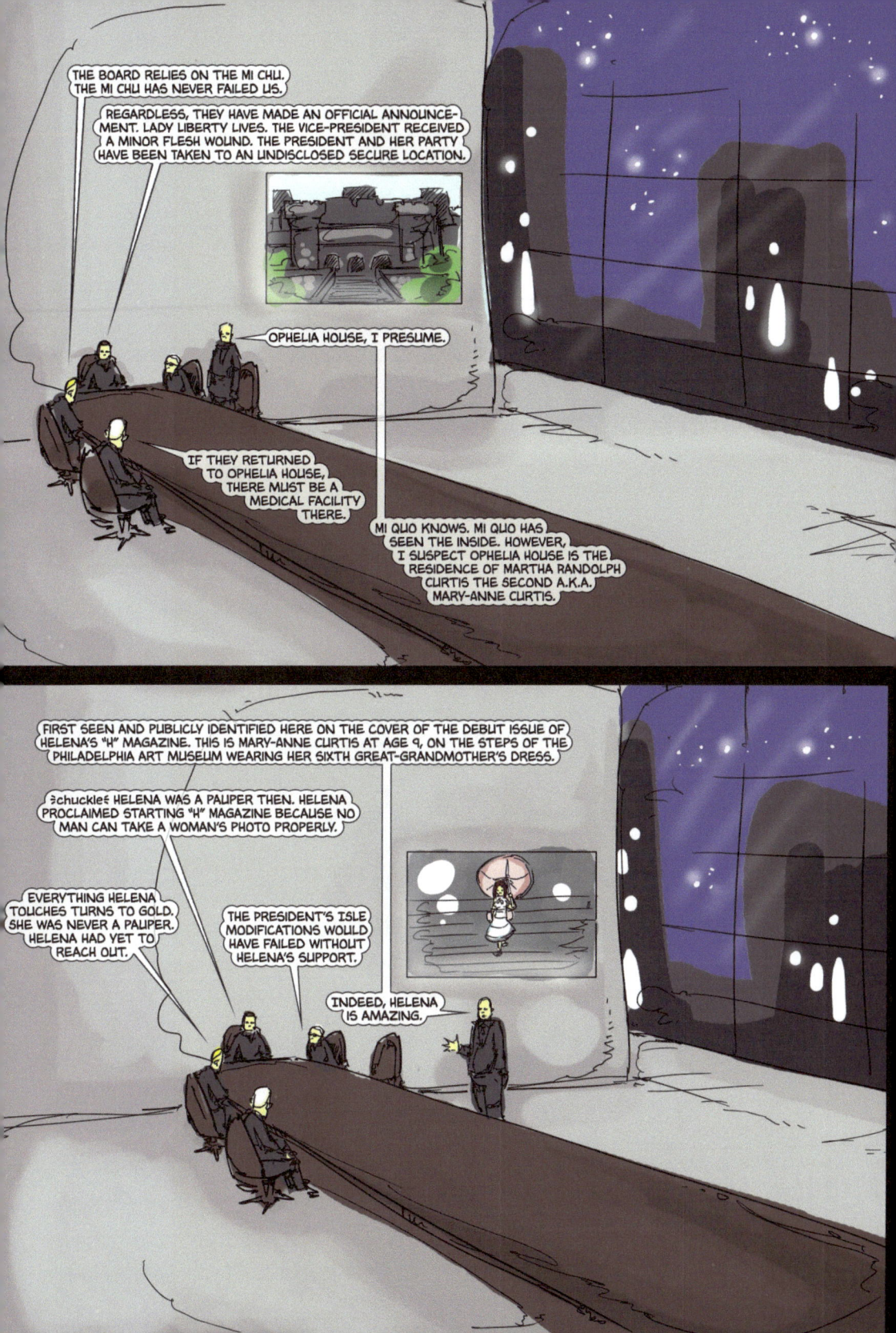

HOWEVER, A MIRACLE, COMPUTER, PEACE VIRUS, A LOGIC BOMB, INFECTED TRANSPORTATION SYSTEMS INTERNATIONALLY WHILE, COINCIDENTLY, MEMBERS OF SELECT PRIVATE FAMILY FORTUNES GATHERED CLANDESTINELY AT MARY-ANNE CURTIS'S RESIDENCE. CURRENTLY A LOCAL DISRUPTION IN THE E.A.I.C. NETWORK OF UNKNOWN ORIGIN IS ISOLATING A SPORTS STADIUM HOLDING AN EVENT MARY-ANNE CURTIS ATTENDS. AND THE MI CHU, THE SECRET DEATH, AN ASSASSIN THAT HAS NEVER FAILED MISSED A TARGET MARY-ANNE CURTIS STOOD NEXT TO.

THE FIELD-TEST OF THE RIFLE SCOPE AT THE ISLE PACIFIC REGION CONFERENCE IN HAWAII PROVED THE RIFLE SCOPE FUNCTIONED PROPERLY.* OBVIOUSLY THE REFLECTIVE GLASS OF THE PRESIDENTIAL BOOTH EXCEEDED THE RIFLE SCOPE'S CAPABILITIES. THE CAUSE OF DISRUPTION IN OUR NETWORK WILL BE IDENTIFIED AND THE PEACE VIRUS WAS A RUSE. YOU SEE COINCIDENCES AND CREATE A CONSPIRACY TO SATISFY YOUR UNCERTAINTY.

THIS IS THE LAST IMAGE OF MARY-ANNE CURTIS WE RECEIVED FROM VETERANS STADIUM.

WHAT IS SHE HOLDING?

A TELEPHONE.

IF OPHELIA HOUSE IS MARY-ANNE CURTIS'S RESIDENCE MI QUO MIGHT HAVE MET HER AND BEFRIENDED HER. IT IS MI QUO'S JOB. MI QUO DOES HER JOB QUITE WELL.

I DO NOT LIKE COINCIDENCES AND THOSE EYES ARE NOT DISTURBED. THOSE EYES WORRY ME. MARTHA RANDOLPH CURTIS THE SECOND A.K.A. MARY-ANNE CURTIS WOULD BE A FIERCE ADVERSARY.

I AGREE. AN ADVERSARY TO BE WARY OF.

*PO LYN LEE "OPHELIA HOUSE" EPISODE 3 "LADY LIBERTY" PAGE 30 - 31

≥ssssss≤

≥squahiss≤

≥ssssss≤

≥squahiss≤

≥squahiss≤

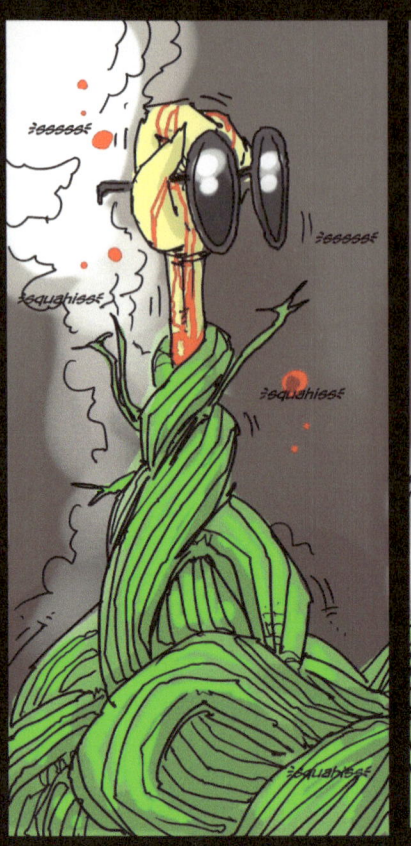

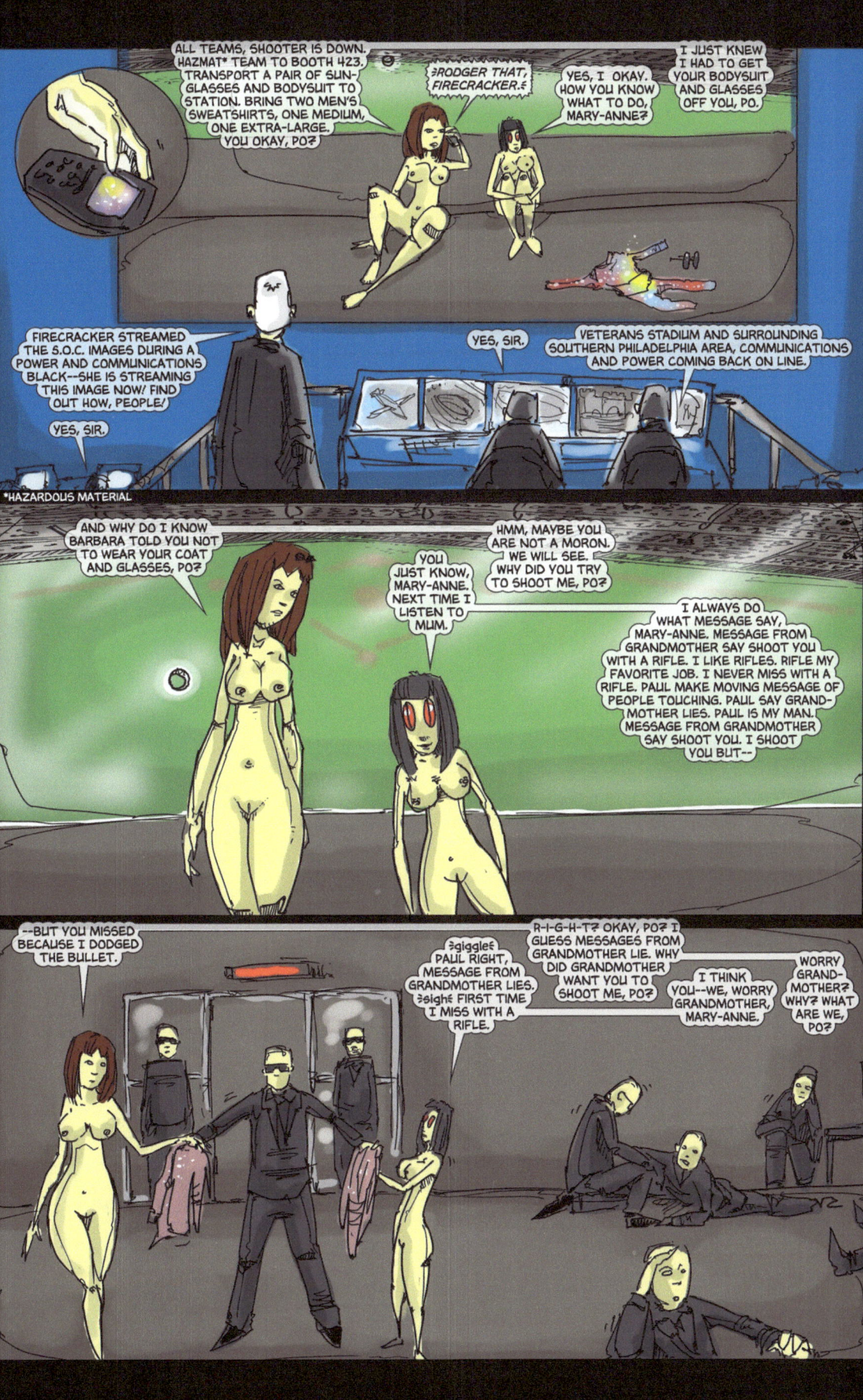

*HAZARDOUS MATERIAL

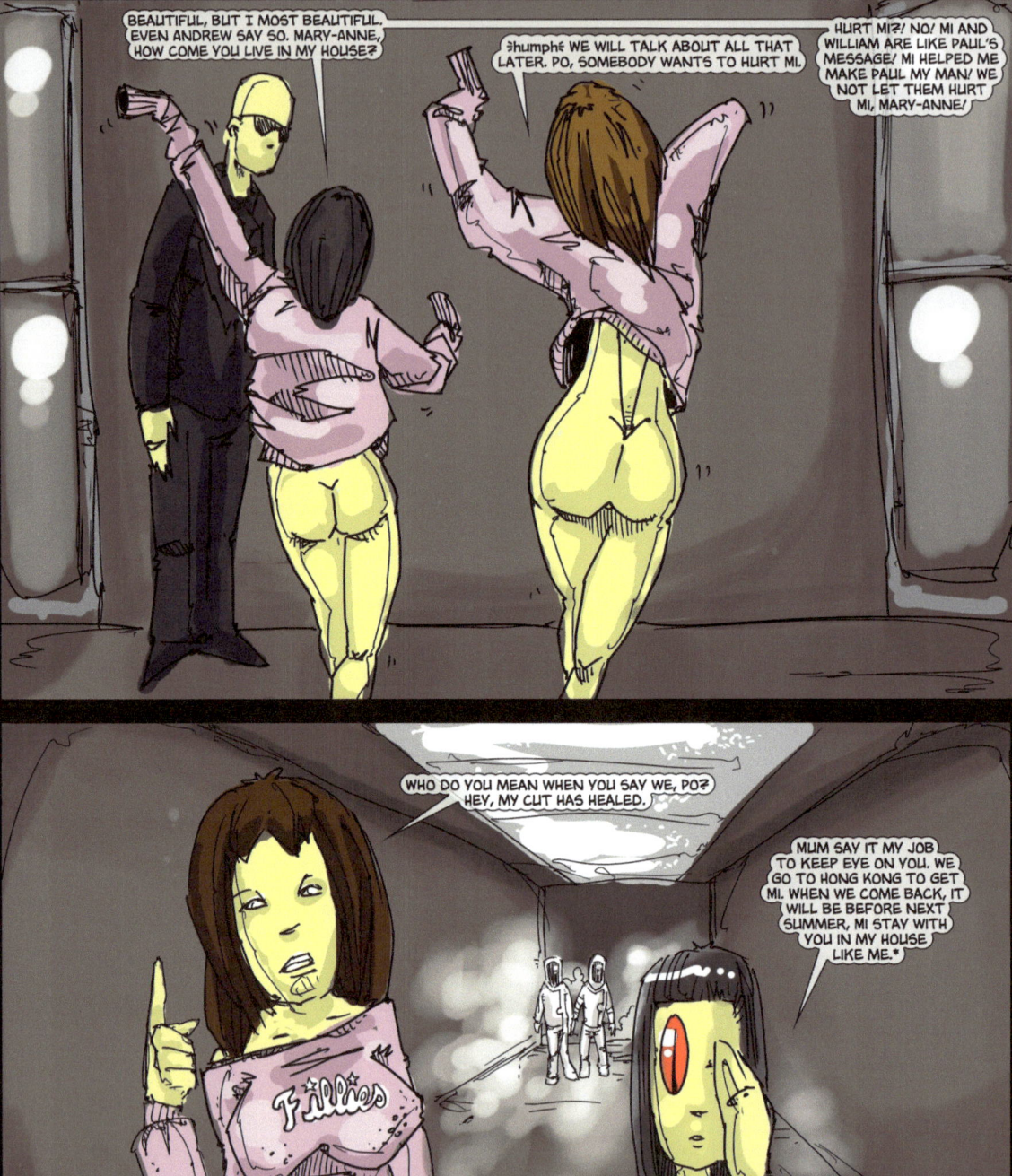

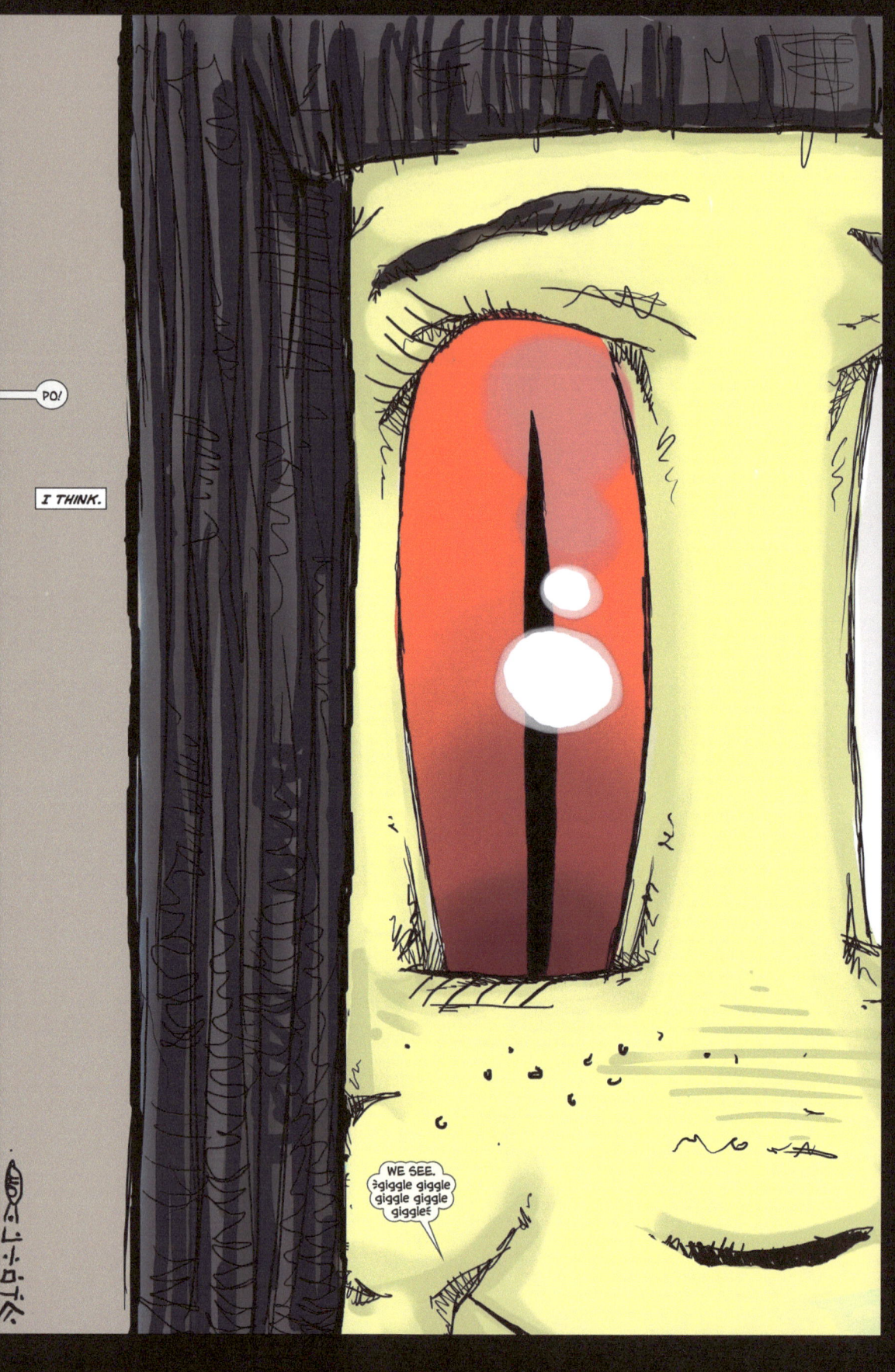

PO LYN LEE

NEXT BOOK

"DEMONS BROOD"

FAMILY REUNIONS TIE UP LOOSE ENDS AND
ISSUES OF THE PAST SURVIVED BY THE AVATAR
AND MI CHU. THE COURSE PI LYN CHARTED
FOR THE SIRYN EMPYREAN AND SCRIBED ON
TA SHEN LING PARCHMENT DID NOT TURN
OUT RIGHT ACCORDING TO THE MESSAGE
GRANDMOTHER COMPOSED AS PO'S LAST
JOB. IT IS A CAGEY SITUATION FOR MI QUO
AND WILLIAM CURTIS, WHO HAVE THE
PLEASURE OF MEETING SIN PANG. THE SEA
LEVEL IS RISING AND PANG LI'S SHIP IS IN HONG
KONG. BELIEF, SOME SAY LORE, IS MORE THAN
JUST A PASSING FANTASY FROM THE PAST;
IT IS A STREET FAIR FOR CARNIVORES WHEN
A PROPER RELIGION COMES TO TOWN.

CARLTON L. SAMPSON

POET, GRAPHIC NOVEL AUTHOR
CARLTON@POLYNLEE.COM
OTHER WORK AVAILABLE AT:
WWW.PHASCISTCLOWNS.COM

ANDREW L. WILLIS

AKA, THIOBIS THE ARTIST
FINE ART, SCULPTURE, ANIMATION,
MUSIC, AND LITERURE.
ANDREW@POLYNLEE.COM
OTHER WORK AVAILABLE AT:
WWW.WAOOBAKEARTWORK.COM

CHEK LAP KOK
HONG KONG
INTERNATIONAL
AIRPORT

FAMILY REUNIONS TIE UP LOOSE ENDS AND
ISSUES OF THE PAST SURVIVED BY THE AVATAR
AND MI CHU. THE COURSE PI LYN CHARTED
FOR THE SIRYN EMPYREAN AND SCRIBED ON
TA SHEN LING PARCHMENT DID NOT TURN
OUT RIGHT ACCORDING TO THE MESSAGE
GRANDMOTHER COMPOSED AS PO'S LAST JOB.
IT IS A CAGEY SITUATION FOR MI QUO AND
WILLIAM CURTIS, WHO HAVE THE PLEASURE
OF MEETING SIN PANG. THE SEA LEVEL IS
RISING AND PANG LI'S SHIP IS IN HONG KONG.
BELIEF, SOME SAY LORE, IS MORE THAN
JUST A PASSING FANTASY FROM THE PAST;
IT IS A STREET FAIR FOR CARNIVORES WHEN
A PROPER RELIGION COMES TO TOWN.

NEXT BOOK

"DEMONS BROOD"

WWW.POLYNLEE.COM

www.ingramcontent.com/pod-product-compliance
Lightning Source LLC
Chambersburg PA
CBHW041537240626
47164CB00002B/41